CONFESSIONS OF A SOCIOPATHIC SOCIAL CLIMBER

Also by Adèle Lang: *How to Spot a Bastard by His Star Sign*

Confessions of a Sociopathic Social Climber

The Katya Livingston Chronicles

Adèle Lang

THOMAS DUNNE BOOKS
St. Martin's Press   New York

THOMAS DUNNE BOOKS.
An imprint of St. Martin's Press.

www.stmartins.com

ISBN 0-312-28811-5

First published in Great Britain by Mainstream Publishing Company
(Edinburgh) Ltd under the title *What Katya Did Next: Chronicles of a
Sociopathic Social Climber.*

10 9 8 7 6 5 4

*In memory of George Smith, and to his beloved wife, Isabel,
for creating a life that has never failed to inspire me.*

ACKNOWLEDGMENTS

Thanks to Fiona Brownlee, Susi Rajah, Jennifer Reeve, Carin Siegfried, and Thomas Dunne for helping an undesirable like Katya gain admittance into America; to Bill Campbell, Anne Dewe, Deborah Gray, and Russell Taylor for ensuring she didn't get thrown out of Britain either; to Jane Burridge, Timothy Gill, Jonathan Green, Andrew Masterson, Jane Palfreyman, Matthew Quick, Margaret Sullivan, and Alison Urquhart for ensuring she got a good start in Australia before finally being deported; and to this author's long-suffering parents, along with her equally long-suffering Ex (he knows who he is) for coming to mine (and Katya's) international rescue time and time again.

Also, thanks to this author's ongoing travelling companions: Jessica Adams, Maria Barr, Nick Blyth, James Brown, Carole-Anne Burton, Colin Cameron, Leesa Candeloro, Lana Citron, Halide Dale, Michelle Davies, Mark Dawson, Steve Deput, Justine Ettler, Jan and Bryan Ferguson, Leigh Ferrani, Tim France, Alison Fraser, Gus Guillen, Sophia Hesselgren, Nigel Lang, Tim Lawler, Ayla Master, Christina Mitsis, Rachel Oakes-Ash, Hazel Persaud, Susi Rajah (again), Louise Sersansie, Elaine Sharp, Trevor Smith, Tara Spring, Zora Suleman, Bina Tarulli, Russell Taylor (again), Kate Tierney, Angela Taylor, Clifford Thurlow, and Anna-Louise Weatherley. Unlike Katya, you guys deserve to go far.

PROLOGUE

Monday   **1 July**

Clearly unaware that unlike his good self, I've got a thriving career, a frantic social calendar and a very promising love life, my accountant has advised me to keep this stupid financial diary because he thinks I'm likely to get harassed again by distrusting civil servants from the Inland Revenue. As I was quick to point out when I went to visit him this morning at England's most reputable open prison, it doesn't take a recently struck-off International Chartered Accountants member to leap to that startling conclusion – particularly after last year's fiasco. Thanks to my accountant's inability to lie convincingly enough under oath on my behalf in the High Court, I was lumbered with huge fines for undeclared earnings and over-claimed business expenses.

To make matters worse, when I got back to the ad agency where I work, I found out that Suzette, my art director partner of just two weeks, has managed to wrangle her way out of her watertight work contract by telling anyone who'd listen that I've inspired her to 'find God' in South America. For a moment I was quite flattered to hear this news from my furious, puce-faced boss when he stormed into my office after a meeting with his agency's solicitors. Then he nastily went on to say that what Suzette meant was she'd rather pursue penniless aid work in Brazil than stay put in a well-paying job in London alongside me. Personally, I think Suzette's just jealous because I'm underweight for my height and I've never been caught buying eye gel from budget outlets like the Body Shop. Plus, I own a Prada bag and she doesn't.

Proceed to rummage round Suzette's now-abandoned desk in search of the slimming tablets I loaned her last week, and which she very obviously never bothered to use. Am subsequently appalled to discover a half-written letter to the Inland Revenue. It seems that after all I've done for her, the ungrateful cow was planning to shop me for misappropriating her Greenpeace newsletter receipts for the last financial quarter. Briefly consider placing hoax bomb threats to all international carriers en route to Rio, but opt instead for stealing her ergonomic chair since the hydraulics on my own went kaput after an exceptionally unprofessional petting session with our ad agency's power-tool client at last year's Christmas party.

Business Expenses: *Accountant's Fee – £10 (as decreed by the Trade Practices in Prison Act, 2001); Hand-bound vellum diary – £90; Mt Blanc Pen – £250. (At this rate, will have to get a second job to subsidise the expensive lifestyles of so-called 'fiscal experts' who specialise in sucking my bank account dry.)*

Tuesday   2 July

As luck would have it, amateur literary hack (and professional barman at the Coach & Horses in Soho) Teddington rings me up at work this morning. He's all in a lather because he thinks he's found his 'big break'. Apparently his mentor, a dispatch boy at *London Goss**, has told him the editor there is looking for a 'talented young unknown' to write a weekly social diary, and is willing to pay handsomely for the privilege.

Since Teddington is neither talented nor young, save him from the unnecessary humiliation and rejection that is sure to follow, and apply for the job myself. Tear the first day's page out of this diary and send it to the *London Goss* editor, along with a photo of me sunbathing in a fetching one-piece bikini in St Tropez last summer.

Satisfied with my day's toil thus far, tackle my boss about the whereabouts of my new art director because there's no way I'm going to carry the agency workload by myself. Collar him as he's sneaking back to his office from the men's room, no doubt having slipped a few sly snifters of the Chivas Regal he keeps stashed in the paper-towel dispenser. He proceeds to make up some pathetic excuse about how no one will work with me as I have garnered a reputation as a 'prima donna'. In a fit of pique, trash his in-tray, kick the legs on his Queen Anne desk, all the while screaming that considering being a highly strung, extremely precious, megalomaniacal, manic-depressive drama queen is a prerequisite to being an advertising copywriter, I can't see how I stand out in particular.

Satisfied I've made my point clear, stomp back to my own

* *Name changed to protect the author from professional embarrassment.*

office and put a call through to the only headhunter in town who's not in a meeting and insist she find me another job.

Business Expenses: None. All job-hunting activities made during company time and at the company's expense.

Wednesday   3 July

Get into work three hours late in protest of my boss's unreasonable behaviour yesterday and immediately ring headhunter to find out why I haven't been swamped with job offers. She starts apologising feebly, and says she is having to put out feelers overseas because she can't place me anywhere here as my reputation has 'preceded me'. My indignation and disgust know no limits after hearing this travesty of justice, I'd presumed most London ad agencies would be honoured to have me on board.

Too upset to do any work, so head to Bar Italia for the afternoon. Spot token, platonic male friend Ferguson, sitting on his lonesome nursing his nose. As one of the few men in London who doesn't need a dribble bowl in my presence, it goes without saying that Ferguson is a rampant homosexual – so much so he's now employed by a high-class escort agency that caters for men of all predilections. But, as I remind him over several vats of Beaujolais, he makes for a completely useless gigolo. Falling in love with the clients and having to bribe them with money so they'll keep on seeing him is bad enough; frittering away what profits he does make on vain attempts to look as good as me is begging for public derision en masse.

Business Expenses: None. Ferguson paid for drinks after I very falsely complimented him on his disastrous new nose job which he's just had done to help him get over Dwight, his latest ex-client.

Thursday   4 July

My mother, who lives in Barnsley, has sent a tub of life-enhancing, vile-tasting powdered seaweed to my office by first-class mail, claiming she is worried about my health. She doesn't understand that being a physical wreck is part of the perks of careerdom. Nor does she seem to care that I'm having a hard enough time trying to quell last night's Beaujolais without her adding to my problems.

Put the unsolicited jar of plankton into the Oxfam collection box I find stashed under Suzette's desk. Then take it out again because, really, the hungry and homeless shouldn't have to suffer any more than absolutely necessary. Decide, instead, to put it back where it originally came from and surreptitiously pour it into the art deco fish tank that sits in our agency foyer wasting valuable space along with the Gatekeeper who mans the switchboard at front desk and listens in on all my calls.

Then take an extra-early lunch break with Eliza, the hopeless hippy who works in accounts, whom I am only friends with because I feel sorry for her. No female, no matter how shockingly plain, deserves to suffer the ignominy of not having had a boyfriend for three years purely because every male in town knows about the Curse of Namambo hanging over her homely head. (A true story Eliza told me three years ago about how, when she went to the West Indies to study voodoo cults, a raddled old crone took offence at being stereotyped by ignorant British tourists and pointed a bone at her, declaring that, from there on out, any man brave enough to try and befriend Eliza would meet a grisly end.)

Eliza takes me to some godforsaken Soho cesspit that prides itself on its distressed furniture and thoroughly unphotogenic hired help. Without a single trace of irony, Eliza says it makes her feel at home. The place must have something going for it though, as all the style vultures are there, fishing cigarette butts out of their long machiattos. While I dust the table down with a pre-used napkin, Eliza prattles on about how she's been reading *The Celestine Prophecy* during office hours, and is now training to be a 'guide'. Privately, I worry all the bad karma and horrific hexes surrounding her may project on to her customers' auras. She guilelessly offers to practise on me, but I wilfully beg off by saying I'm an atheist.

Arrive back at agency in late afternoon and spy the Gatekeeper scooping the boss's prized Japanese koi out of the fish tank because they've all started to float belly-up in the water.

Business Expenses: None. Eliza paid for brunch, lunch and afternoon tea because she's grateful I'll be seen with her in public.

Friday   5 July

Taking advantage of the fact the Gatekeeper has been ordered by my boss to reluctantly use her trade-unionised, office-clerk, 60-minute lunch-break to transfer water samples from the fish tank to a local chemist to find out what killed his koi, intercept incoming mail and open all correspondence addressed to Suzette – since she's no longer here to do it herself. One letter's from Sabelo, her World Vision sponsor child. Reading between the lines, because I can't actually decipher the words above and below, I learn that Sabelo is eight years old, lives in a hut in one of South Africa's less salubrious suburbs and lists 'eating' as his favourite hobby. After a lengthy chat with my incarcerated accountant, impulsively decide to become Sabelo's foster parent. Pen an immeasurably more well-versed letter back to my latest acquisition, advising him of the sudden change in payment plans. Also take care to detail my brilliant career, fabulous social life and excellent money prospects and request that Sabelo write back to me posthaste so I've got proof of purchase. Since my accountant waived his usual pro rata prison rates this time, so touched was he to hear about my first tentative step into philanthropy, feel slightly more benevolent than usual and enclose a little gift which I found lying around in the stationery cupboard.

Business Expenses: Charitable donation to starving child – £0 (Suzette's already paid through until November); charitable gift (Oxford Dictionary) – £0.

Saturday   6 July

Don't have to go to work today so get up early. Virtuously visit King's Road to buy a home-office heater because it's tax-deductible and I'm freezing in London's typically brisk summer weather. Of course, since I have to pass entire racks of clothes to get to Dixons, it's not my fault when I arrive home with things that refuse to resemble heating appliances, even if I could be bothered to solder plugs on to them and set them alight. Spend afternoon cursing my

fickleness, wrapped in blanket and eating Ritz biscuits straight
from the box because my kitchen is too cold to stand still in one
spot long enough to find a clean plate.

Later, make herculean leap from bed to bath to brand-new
Joseph suit as I'm meeting with Phoebe at the Met Bar as her
boyfriend has to spend Saturday nights with his wife. Like most
women d'un certain age, old Phoebe thinks dating a married man,
and then banging on about the loneliness of it all to her hapless
friends, is better than not having a date at all. So, whilst she weeps
softly every time she spots a happy couple canoodling in the
corner, I have to amuse myself by watching the antics of a bottle-
blond, surfie type who I'm sure used to be in *Home and Away* but
is now getting pissed with all his other out-of-work friends. To my
absolute horror, I suddenly realise that one of them is my thespian
ex; and he's standing well within two hundred metres of me.
Although the restraining order I put out on him doesn't expire
until next month, I allow my jilted lover to buy me a few rounds of
Absolut – though only on the proviso he does a couple of
maintenance jobs around my flat afterwards.

Business Expenses: *Clothes for promotional purposes – £600.*

Sunday   7 July

With much dramatic flourish, boot my ex out of bed in the early
morning and make him mend my kitchen tap as promised.
Symbolically, tap is completely stuffed. Out of pity, for I do
understand how hard it is for former graduates of Royal Academy
of Dramatic Arts to find work in the real world, set him about
cleaning my floors, dusting my bookshelves and changing my
sheets. Then, after he's also defrosted my fridge-freezer and taken
the rubbish out, Ex throws me a spectacularly unconvincing look
of longing, mutters something about being late for an important
audition* and starts to exit left. Immediately feel guilty so do the
right thing and meekly ask for a reconciliation. Ex says this is
impossible because he loves me madly, can't live without me and
is dating no one else. Knowing him like I do, his reasoning makes

*See Saturday, 13 July.

perfect sense. Nonetheless, feel legally obligated to report his psychotic behaviour to my local police station (I think the sergeant there secretly fancies me because he's always extremely abrupt when I do my weekly phone-in).

Business Expenses: None. Ex did all home-office cleaning for free.

Monday 8 July

Have just been assigned by slightly naive, married male editor to write candid single girl's diary for prestigious tabloid *London Goss*. Afterwards, in minicab (because I don't do public transport), resolve to be gentle with the doddery old fool without compromising my inner bitch who's beside herself at the thought of publicly slagging off every *amoretto* who crosses her from here on in. The typically rude minicab driver interrupts my reverie and asks if he should take up a more lucrative bricklayer's job he's been offered in Essex. Helpfully reply it's up to him. Then he asks me how much I earn. Lie and halve my salary because poor people often react badly when I tell them how much I get paid to write: 'Bread Rolls – 89p a dozen'.

Business Expenses: Have decided to discontinue itemising expenses and documenting business dealings here. Like the rest of the nation, snoops at Inland Revenue can read all about it in my new diary which starts tomorrow in London Goss, *and which I shall start writing after a celebratory quaff of the Krug I've just discovered hidden behind the Budvar in my boss's bar fridge.*

PART I

Tuesday   **9 July**
England's foremost diarist, Katya Livingston, is feeling extremely unwell and would like to apologise to her readers – male or otherwise – for the absence of her debut entry in today's edition of London Goss. *Her much-vaunted column about life in the fast lane will start tomorrow instead.*

Wednesday   **10 July**
Today, whilst taking a cigarette break in the office lift (because smoking has been banned in the office building), spot potential breeder. I think he works for the computer data processing company on the fourth floor. He's got an exotic northern European accent ('*Rygning forbudt i elevatoren*') and a thunderous look on his face. So from now on I shall call him Thor.

Heart beating wildly, breathlessly make my way out of the lift into the ad agency, ruing the day I switched from Marlboro Lights to Marlboro Reds. Heart nearly stops altogether at the sight of my boss in the foyer: jowly face livid with anger and too much drinking before office hours, he's just been informed by a baffled chemist that the koi in the fish tank were poisoned. Typically, he's decided to blame me. Put out by his predictable prejudice, I shriek like a banshee, threaten to smash the Damien Hirst that hangs behind the Gatekeeper's desk and ask if I look like someone who'd intentionally kill a harmless fish. My boss gives me a peculiar look but drops the subject quickly enough.

Back at my desk, receive further inflammatory comments by way of a call from perpetually failing writer, Teddington. Unaware of my recent appointment at *London Goss*, because he can't afford to buy a newspaper, Teddington mournfully informs me that due to the new mystery columnist's allegedly excessive pay demands, the paper's human resources budget had to be cut and so his erstwhile mentor and dispatch boy, plus 30 other employees, have just been made redundant.

Thursday   **11 July**
Haven't seen Thor again, even though I've taken to taking the lift

on a quarter-hourly basis in order to bump into him. Then, on my 4.15 p.m. shift, walk into my fog-filled hunting ground and there stands my beloved, coughing and wheezing and glowering intensely at the mounting pile of butts on the floor. Overcome by unfamiliar shyness, put my head down and scurry straight out again doing a brilliant impersonation of a Brontë. Therefore, can't say for sure if he was watching me with dark and brooding eyes.

Friday   **12 July**
Don't get much work done as I'm daydreaming about Thor. Sadly, he doesn't yet know he's the object of massive lust and longing and will one day will be the father of my children; and neither is he likely to, thanks to some spoilsport office cleaner who grassed to the building's security firm and had me banned from smoking in the lift and reduced to puffing in the fire-exit stairwell instead. At my insistence, plain but pliant Eliza from accounts volunteers to find out Thor's real name. Whilst I breathe heavily down her office phone extension, she anonymously calls the computer data processing company's receptionist and pretends someone there rang her about a business matter but she can't quite recall his name though: '*he did have a rather exotic northern European accent,*' I hiss.

Helpful receptionist says the company employs several foreigners. Of course, Eliza (nor, indeed, I) can hardly then say, '*the drop-dead gorgeous one, stupid,*' since Eliza's only meant to have talked to him over the phone. To add to my woes and keep me apart from Thor forever, the Gatekeeper joins our conference call and, in excessively insinuating tones, says 'Hortense' wants me to call her back. Since this is the rather clever code name my stupid headhunter uses to get past front desk without raising the suspicions of the Gatekeeper,I ring 'Hortense' straight away and berate her for blowing my cover. Headhunter apologises feebly. Then, thinking I'll be pleased to hear this, she says there are several copywriting jobs up for grabs in Singapore. Hang up on her abruptly and vow never to return her calls again until she starts appreciating me more.

Saturday   **13 July**

Endeavour to buy home-office heater again for my flat. Take the long route to Dixons in order to detour King's Road's beckoning boutiques and, instead, get lured into all those everything-for-a-quid shops. End up shoplifting three hair-clips, six napkin rings, one bottle of green nail polish and still no heater.

Afterwards, and only because I can eat junk food and still remain smooth-complexioned, head off to procure a Big Mac, medium fries and small Coke. To my complete and utter embarrassment, catch my thespian ex (who likes large cokes, with straw) dressed in the corporate clown suit. He, too, seems utterly abashed at being caught looking like a total idiot. Again. We briefly reminisce about the time I beat his acting peers at charades whilst he was in the bathroom blowing his nose. Conversation is mercifully cut short by a four-year-old who wants 'Ronald's' autograph. Am assured by nearby youth piling burgers on to trays that I looked suitably alluring, yet massively unattainable throughout.

In evening, was supposed to be meeting with Phoebe but she bowed out at very last minute, saying she's too distressed because she's just read that only one out of ten married men leave their wives. So, instead, stay in and call local police station and inform the smitten sergeant that my ex has now taken to stalking me in public places. Perhaps jealous of the persistent attentions I am getting from another man, my sergeant rather brusquely says he'll get on to the case as soon as he's captured the serial rapist who's presently terrorising my neighbourhood.

Sunday   **14 July**

Knowing full well he can't bear the thought of anyone else sleeping with me, ring Ex and demand he come round and deadlock all the windows in my flat to protect me from the marauder in my midst. Never any good at ad-libbing at the best of times, Ex makes poorly rehearsed apologetic noises and says he can't because he's got to prepare for a very demanding character role,* oblivious to the fact that time – let alone Katya – waits for no man. Anyway, I've already

*See Friday, 27 December.

worked out a way to deter Mr Serial Rapist. If he does come knocking on my door, I'm going to ask him for a commitment. That should send him fleeing into the night.

Nevertheless, by early evening start feeling sorry for myself so trot off to the Atlantic Bar and mingle with menopausal trendies just for a laugh. Get hideously drunk on bar tabs, other than mine, distribute business cards indiscriminately and make lots of unhappily married men happy in the process.

Monday   15 July

Spend all morning at work fending off phone calls resulting from last night's escapades, even I refuse to accept dates from men whose physical appearance I can't recall because I was too blind drunk at the time. Come noon, and face even redder than usual, boss stormtroops into my office and informs me that a telly commercial I recently shot has just been rejected by our used-car sales client who fears that using a low-rent slapper to sell second-hand goods might be bad for his image. This news doesn't impress me much for I'm trying to get as many controversial ads to air as possible so I can be catapulted to adland infamy and accompanying enormous pay cheque.

To cheer myself up at lunchtime, drag Eliza from accounts into the café next door to letch at Thor, my Scandinavian love-god. Have to grab seats in the no-smoking section for a vantage view. Whilst Thor waves away the smoke from my cigarette, hawk-eyed Eliza points out the narrow gold band on his ring finger on his left hand. That's it. It's over. I don't mate with married men. It's so desperate. And besides, I'm sick to death of sitting in sleazy pick-up joints and being regaled about wayward kids, unresponsive wives and expensive baby-sitters. Plus there's nothing romantic about watching grown men scream blue murder when you deliberately give them lovebites their spouses will spot.

Tuesday   16 July

Spend all day locked away in a Soho sound studio, recording a radio ad that's a bit derogatory to the Welsh. Anyway, I'm sure taffy types are used to jokes about how they like to shag sheep. And, as I assured my doubtful boss this morning when I finally relented and let him see the script five minutes before recording started, if they don't like it, they can stop sponging off hard-working tax-paying English people like myself and naff off back to their fourth-rate peninsula. After many frustrating hours trying to get a ewe to bleat on cue, return to agency to find another message from 'Hortense' the headhunter beseeching me to call.

Wednesday **17 July**
Have had to contract convincing and life-threatening Asian flu for the benefit of my boss because I've got to fly to Singapore tonight for a job interview. Have no intention of working in a third-world country but decide to take the trip because I'm being flown business class. Call the Gatekeeper and tell her to tell my boss that I won't be in today as I'm very, very sick. She replies it's probably just pre-job interview jitters but to have a nice trip all the same. Hang up on her in utter disgust.

After spending pleasant enough hours compiling my comprehensive duty-free list, arrive at executive lounge at Heathrow. Unaccustomed to corporate etiquette, stuff myself with free wine and canapés whilst counting my blessings that I'm still a recovering bulimic. On the plane, get harangued by Attila the Hostess for accidentally crossing the curtain to use the economy-class loos. I, in turn, tick her off for wearing too much make-up on the job. She informs me it's regulation uniform. This might be so, I reply sardonically, but only youthful types such as myself can get away with wearing five layers of Mac under harsh cabin lighting.

Thursday **18 July**
Arrive in Singapore, eyeballs hanging out of head. Am singularly unimpressed with the city or, indeed, its inhabitants. Like I said to a particularly unswerving and surprisingly short member of the Singapore police force I met outside the airport's main entrance, it's all very well and good toting oneself as a modern-day metropolis and cleanest city in Asia, but slapping a ginormous fine

on an exceptionally tall and attractive female foreigner for absent-mindedly tossing a few duty-free shopping bags on to the street in her haste to get to her cut-price Marlboros is completely barbaric.

Proceed to spend rest of morning feeling like Gulliver and trying not to step on my Lilliputian potential employer who is endeavouring to convince me that Singapore is a nice place to visit. During lunch at a five-star restaurant, he expects me to eat real Cantonese food that's still trying to crawl off my plate. After that he takes me to Raffles for a decidedly ho-hum gin sling and proudly informs me that Somerset Maugham once shot a tiger in the billiard room. I sharply retort that he probably meant to shoot one of the liveried Oompah-Loompahs for skimping on the Gordon's.

Then, knowing full well I haven't had sleep for over two days and one night, my potential employer tries to make me sign a two-year contract on the spot. After squinting at the small print, decide there's no way I'm going to work a five-and-a-half day week even if I get paid ten times the squillions he's threatening to throw at me. But, scared he'll cancel my free flight home, smile fatuously, nod my head a lot, and promise to buy *Expatriates Living in Singapore* at the airport bookshop tonight.

Friday   19 July
Go straight from airport to advertising agency and arrange myself in a life-like position behind my desk. Woken from my slumber in late afternoon by my boss who is fair purple with apoplexy. Apparently, my radio ad about a Welshman's fondness for sheep has just been rejected by our woollen undergarments client who is worried about complaints from the RSPCA. Too tired to care or to dream up a clever comeback.

Saturday   20 July
Arise early evening because I've promised to meet foppish Ferguson at a Bermondsey bar after he's finished working the Canary Wharf. Don't really want to be here as this is Ex's haunt and we agreed I would stay away so he could get over me quicker. So, as Ferguson drones on about the City banker who mistook him

for a girl because of all the blusher he's been wearing to hide a recently botched acid peel, I keep a furtive eye on the door in case Ex walks in and beats up the barman who's been staring at me for longer than is polite and who Ferguson reckons is cross-eyed and is really staring at him.

Sunday   21 July

Now I'm a celebrated columnist, feel obliged to attend wine-and-cheese meet-and-greet hosted by *London Goss* and put on especially for me. Am therefore sitting in some Forte hotel, ignoring the many black looks from various members of press who, no doubt, blame me for the paper's most recent cost-cutting exercise.

Things start looking up when my editor taps me on the shoulder and says he wants to introduce me to a fan. My distress is palpable when I discover she's female and she's got a disgusting crewcut with matching overalls and big clumpy boots. She gruffly tells me her name is Sophie, she's a landscape gardener, she writes the *London Goss* horticultural column and she'd love to catch up for drinks some time. Eventually relent and give her my phone number because I figure if we ever do go out together, there's no way we'll both fancy the same person.

Monday   22 July

Struggling scribe Teddington rings up and, in faltering tones, makes a truly pathetic attempt at telling me off for absconding with his 'big break'. His long-suffering girlfriend and completely useless muse (if his writing is anything to go by) treated him to a copy of *London Goss* so he finally got to read my by-line. He informs me that what I did wasn't very 'friendly'. I, quite rightly, point out that since he insists upon dressing out of Salvation Army shops and drinking Bulgarian wine out of a cardboard box, I don't think he actually qualifies as one of my friends.

Tuesday   23 July

Horrendously trying day at work, thanks to the fact my computer keyboard had a breakdown so I couldn't actually do any.

Wednesday   24 July

Still refusing to write any ads without the aid of a computer. Instead, spend most of the day translating a letter I've just received from Sabelo, my World Vision waif. I must say, his spelling is coming on in leaps and bounds. He asks me if it's true that if he stopped listening to do-gooder missionary types and instead took a more materialistic approach to life, he too could earn nearly as much money as me?

Write a warm and heartfelt letter back to my late-blooming scholar and enclose a copy of *Running a Small Business for Fun and Profit* which I found carelessly hidden in my employer's private safe.

Thursday   25 July

Days of sloth end when my computer keyboard comes back from the repairers in the late afternoon. Apparently, it was the dirtiest one the mechanics had ever come across. Some 'wit' wrote technical report as follows: *Keyboard has been thoroughly cleaned and sterilised. Half a gram of tobacco or other substance was carefully removed and rolled, and subsequently smoked. No noticeable or pleasurable effect was recorded.*

Friday   26 July

Still no signs of my boss relenting and hiring a lackey for me to ease my workload. Neither will he give me compassionate leave on the grounds that I'm exhausted. Indeed, when I collar him on his way to the loo today, he says it's about time I 'earned my keep'. Curtly remind him that I could earn triple what he's paying me at a less tight-wad agency and, indeed, have been approached by such a place. Can't be sure for certain since the lights in the men's loos have blown again, but I think my boss must have blanched from rare to medium-rare upon hearing this little bombshell.

Saturday   27 July

Me and Eliza do an impromptu *Thelma and Louise* today and hit the M4 in search of Brad Pitt lookalikes in Glastonbury. Of course, the way Eliza drives, we're not likely to even career off a cliff let alone bonk a farm boy by lunchtime. When Eliza's clapped-out old VW finally beetles into the town centre, she suggests we book in for obligatory spa with complimentary essential oils. Eliza selects jasmine and rose for her carbuncles and boils, making me secretly glad we're not sharing baths. I, in turn, choose lemongrass for some ethnic cleansing and lavender for the thrush that will inevitably follow. Then spend the next 20 minutes as far away from the revolting bubbly brown dishwater as possible, and even manage to jam my head in the open spa window in a drastic attempt to avoid being asphyxiated by the heady bouquet. Rescued 20 minutes later by a kindly attendant and carried to the massage-room whereby a rather well-built thug asks me which bits I'd like worked on. Resist obvious lewd retort, and proffer my neck and shoulders instead as they're a bit stiff following the débâcle in the spa.

Forty-five minutes later, and a Grievous Bodily Harm-charge pending, crawl out of the restful, relaxing retreat, looking and feeling like death. Eliza wanders off in search of healing crystals whilst I wearily scour town for a public gathering place that won't lynch me for lighting up. End up nursing vodka, lime and soda in the local pub with all the other fed-up London visitors.

Sunday   **28 July**
Spend morning tripping over toddlers on the main street and running amok in markets and galleries, desperately trying to offload some tourist pounds. There are heaps of things masquerading as art and crafts in Glastonbury but, tragically, none will ever get wall or shelf space at my place.

Naturally, non-purveyor of good taste Eliza proceeds to fill her car with hemp-woven placemats, wire candlesticks and a papier mâché toilet-roll holder – the last-named she insultingly, and unsuccessfully, tries to fob off on to me as an early Christmas present.

Barely able to distinguish reality from fantasy at the best of times, Eliza then suggests we go traipse round Salisbury Plains. Whilst she packs a picnic lunch for two, I engineer spectacular disappearing act by hitching my skirt a little further than is legally decent in order to attract the attentions of a speeding lorry driver. Get back to London in record time.

Monday   29 July

After another gruelling day at the ad agency trying to get my *London Goss* column filed, my boss, dressed in Armani penguin suit, and me clad in discreet sequins, go to watch greyhound races in an outer suburb. Our attire is his idea of impressing our agency's fleece-lined-tracksuits client who kindly invited us. Personally, I think the latter would be just as gobsmacked if we'd rocked up in our work clothes. Upon alighting from the limo my boss hired especially for occasion, we're let in immediately by track officials (they think we're with the band) and then herded into the VIP section which is segregated from the seething mass of humanity by what looks like office partitioning. Quickly get into the spirit of things, quaff a cup of sparkling wine, attempt to keep down a mini pork pie and notice that the rabbit is racing round the track so fast the hounds would be hard-pressed to chase it on four wheels, let alone on four legs. At the end of each race, congratulate some of the winning dog-owners. All of them scrape their heads on the nylon carpet, so overcome are they by such an important person gracing their track.

Tuesday   30 July

Decide to grow my nails, so bite them all off to give them head start. This is all the fault of work. Without the aid of an art director, am expected to write a press ad in less than eight hours and be expected to look immaculately groomed – just to perpetuate the myth that the advertising industry is full of idiot bimbos who have nothing better to do than French-manicure their nails.

Later, whilst adding a quick lick of top coat, my boss comes jackbooting into my office waving this morning's edition of *London Goss*. He asks me if it's true I feigned flu last week in order to go for a job interview in Singapore.

Herein lies the problem of being an honest person who works in advertising and writes columns on the side. It's also the reason why I am forced to deny his accusation vehemently, telling him he shouldn't believe everything he reads in the paper. Particularly with my by-line on it.

Wednesday   **31 July**
Boss foolishly thinks that by presenting me with an analogue mobile the size of a standard-issue public telephone box he'll be able to keep tabs on me more easily. Thank him in a suitably sincere manner, switch it off and lug it home. Then heave it into my loft out of harm's reach because I don't want ear cancer.

Thursday   **1 August**
The restraining order I'd put out on my ex has just expired. Am not too happy about this as I suspect I'll no longer appear such an attractive option now that I'm so easy to access again. Unfortunately, when I tried to make moves to stop complacency setting in early this morning, my purported 'admirer' at the local police station threatened to put out an injunction if I so much as dared to set foot in the Magistrate's Court again with my application renewal. Tenuous hold over Ex thus lost, decide to replace the great big gaping hole in my life. At work, grab a copy of *Loot* and scan the classifieds for a second-hand pot-bellied pig because I've heard they're loyal, affectionate, eat leftover takeaways and, like me, have an abiding hatred of long walks.

Whilst I'm deeply absorbed in my quest for runts of the litter, Eliza buzzes my extension to tell me that my intemperate boss has just lurched out of the accounts office and off to the pub after demanding to see my original work contract, my current salary, my expense-account tally, my sick-leave accruals and my worker's compensation claims* because the company auditors have just informed him that his agency is currently running at a huge loss. What this has got to do with me, I have no idea.

*Legitimate claims being processed at the time of this entry: i) Concussion caused by flying door after putting left-over-from-the-night-before,

home-delivered, foil-wrapped beef vindaloo in agency's microwave; ii)
Repetitive Strain Injury caused by having to constantly key in changes to
controversial scripts as decreed by agency management; iii) Fractured
ankle sustained by tripping over a carelessly placed object during a
business meeting at an out-of-house venue (see Tuesday, 13 August).

Friday   2 August

Have decided against acquiring a pot-bellied pig because my
nurturing instincts are being worn completely thin, no small
thanks to Sabelo, my African charity case. I've just received a stern
rebuke from World Vision in the form of a letter telling me I am
not supposed to display my wealth in an ostentatious manner as it
will make Sabelo 'discontented with his lot'. Considering my little
Luddite lives in a one-room asbestos shack with no water, electricity, gas, phone or dishwasher, I can't see how I can help make
him feel any more disgruntled.

Whilst I fire off a response to this effect to World Vision headquarters, my boss appears in my line of vision. He frogmarches me
into his plush-piled office, then plonks me down on to one of his
genuine Chippendale chairs for guests.

Just as I thought, I'm being blamed for the agency's woes.
Indeed, my boss very belligerently informs me that in order to
keep my job I'm going to have to write some ads that actually get
to see the light of day. Furthermore, he says sternly, I'm to stop
writing my *London Goss* column during office hours.

Personally, I think the auditors should take a closer look at my
sybaritic superior's profligate spending on office furnishings. But,
after sincerely promising him I'll bear his wise words in mind,
immediately make an appointment with our agency's out-of-house
software supplier because, in order to write and then file my
column to *London Goss* in future, I'm going to have to get my
boss's laptop* hooked on to the Internet at home.

On arrival at my flat, the software nerd casually asks me why the
ad agency is willing to supply me with an AppleMac Powerbook, a
modem and the relevant software package free of charge. I look

Since he never seems to use it himself.

him straight in the eye and tell him it's because I'm having to do work after hours in a bid to save my employer's neck. Software nerd nods, satisfied and, no doubt, greatly impressed. End up on World Wide Web swapping insults with a particularly un-repentant cross-dresser from Arkansas (sadloser@cybex.com.us).

Saturday   **3 August**
Grand plan to purchase heater today stymied by Eliza who insists upon taking me to Brixton Market to get my tarot cards read, saying I need something to look forward to in my life. Of course, her selfless deed has nothing whatsoever to do with the fact she wants to get her own future revealed in order to find out if the Curse of Namambo has an expiry date. Much card shuffling and second-guessing later, I am assured by an offensively self-satisfied soothsayer that I am a '*deeply unfulfilled person with many tragic relationships behind me and a frustrated creative spirit that has yet to be unleashed*'.

As I was about to say to Eliza as we head back to the better side of town, I don't need to hand over fifty hard-earned pounds to be told the blindingly obvious. Fortunately, I notice Eliza's ominously set features just in time and guess that her own predictions also erred on the stark and bleak. In an attempt to distract her from deliberately veering off Waterloo Bridge I indulge in some upbeat banter instead and point out potentially brave and fearless swains to her as they go whizzing by in their Ford Fiestas.

Don't go out in the evening as I'm feeling a bit premenstrual and am likely to throw my drinks over the first idiot to approach me.

Sunday   **4 August**
Primrose oil capsules still haven't kicked in, so go with flow of premenstrual tension and ensuing self-pity by watching Robert Carlyle on video. He reminds me of Ex. Except, of course, Ex is slightly taller, can't act for toffee and wouldn't propose to me even if his love life depended on it – which it did. Which is why he hasn't got one any more.

Monday   **5 August**

Spend most of my working day wondering why I haven't got a man. Then stare into my compact mirror and, noticing a particularly hideous blemish on my chin, realise exactly why. Men never notice you're a complete bitch from two hundred metres but they do know a boil when they see one. Boss rudely interrupts my melancholy musings with some work he wants me to do. It's for one of his friends who's trying to sell a stud farm in Newmarket.

When I try to explain that I've got more important things on my mind, he, like most people who are happily married with three children, is totally unsympathetic. 'Write me a masterpiece,' he barks before sloping off to lunch. Do my best and, many minutes later, deliberately slam literary triumph down upon his desk to make a point (a complete waste of time since he's still out to lunch) and stalk out of work at 5.29.59 p.m. precisely, beating the Gatekeeper to the lift.

Get home, kick empty letter box and storm into flat, banging door dramatically just for the benefit of any neighbours who may be male, single and fond of women with attitude.

Tuesday   **6 August**

Am determined to be a much nicer person today. Good intentions slightly impeded when my door-to-door service-wash man turns up late, meaning I get out of bed at 9.30 a.m. for nothing. Still, at 9.35 a.m., throw my dirty clothes at him, smiling brightly, if a little falsely, inwardly vowing that I'm not going to answer the door tomorrow when he arrives with my clean laundry – just so as to muck up his routine and inconvenience him. Patience further tested by my increasingly hard-to-please *London Goss* editor who rings me at work to say that whilst the travails of all my loser friends make for a fascinating read, he'd been led to believe I frequently mingled with the rich and infamous.

Immediately call Ferguson, my on-the-street informant. At a loose end because his regular Tuesday morning client has stood him up and his endoscopic brow lift appointment isn't till noon, Ferguson eagerly dishes up his industry's dirt: allegedly a famous West End actress subsidises her whisky habit by pressing her ample flesh for large sums of money. Naturally, I rush to her defence because I too have been the subject of scurrilous rumours. Ferguson cattily replies that everything he's ever heard said about me behind my back has been true.

Wednesday   7 August

Win this week's celebrity-spotting office sweepstake because our agency is close to a TV production company and me and Eliza like to kill time by trying to brush shoulders with aging news anchors and reptilian game-show hosts. Today I saw a supremely scruffy ex-soap star in the café next door. Given his tendency to collapse in public, I stood behind him, arms outstretched, frantically wishing I'd finished the St John's Ambulance first-aid course I recently started and quit shortly thereafter because of the lack of male members upon which to inflict the kiss-of-life.

Thursday   8 August

Am at the Soho sound studio again, waiting for a much admired British comedian with an exceptionally bad drug habit to show up and record a brilliant and, hopefully, thought-provoking fertiliser advertisement I dreamt up this morning in between applying two-minute conditioner to my hair and then rinsing it out.

Finally stumble across my strung-out star in the men's loo slumped over a wash basin. Smack him about a bit, haul him into the sound booth, prop him up against the mike and thrust the script in front of his pin-pricked eyes. Fortunately my ad comprises only eight words, all of them expletives, so he carries if off fairly well.

Get back to work feeling slightly overwrought from my first-hand experience in the drug wars, only to be greeted by the owner of the stud farm in Newmarket. He's dropped in to rave about the prose I grudgingly wrote on Monday. Thinking he is paying me a massive compliment, he tells me that an old, hardened *estate agent* had tears in his eye after he'd read it.

Friday   **9 August**
Struggling to find any more names to drop for *London Goss,* place an emergency call through to Calliope, my international correspondent. Am consequently appalled to discover that someone has put a lock on my international calls on my phone at work. March through to reception, glare at the Gatekeeper and order her to take it off. She primly replies my boss has given her strict instructions to the contrary. Resist cheap shot at her expense and instead march into my boss's habitually empty office and ring Japan from there.

Calliope is a little disconsolate because she hasn't been frotted on the Tokyo subway yet. I console her by telling her that life is full of disappointments; but at least she can sell her knickers to Japanese businessmen if she gets really desperate. Not that she'll need to. She's earning scads of dough from the commission she gets for emptying vending machines that sell other girls' undies. (It's all part of Calliope's rather long-winded and extremely convoluted plan to become a famous fashion designer and the only reason why I'm bothering to cultivate her friendship – she could still end up being a very valuable contact.)

I ask her if she's seen any celebrities of late. She says she saw an American actor, who allegedly likes small burrowing animals, standing in front of the ferret cage at Tokyo Zoo. Unfortunately, she cannot confirm or deny rumours because he had his back to the bars at the time.

Saturday   **10 August**
Head off for smear test because, during our 72-minute phone conversation yesterday, Calliope told me that women who don't have regular earth-shattering sex are more prone to cervical suffering.

To my horror, discover my non-threatening, fatherly doctor has been replaced by a gorgeous young man – which I'm sure must be against the medical code of ethics. Surreptitiously check my lippie and inwardly kick myself for not wearing my best underwear (which is still with my washing man since I refused to answer the door to him when he showed up with my clean clothes on

Wednesday*). Once on the bed, I'm far too tense to relax and end up getting my blood pressure checked instead. No doubt alarmed at the thought of someone so singularly attractive being cut down in her prime with palpitations, Doctor Love hands me a prescription for sedatives.

Woken from subsequent heavy slumber in early evening by someone called 'Sophie' at the other end of my phone line. '*Sophie who?*' I squeak, terrified that telesales people have at last managed to get hold of my unlisted home number. Sophie explains she's the gardening guru I met at the Forte hotel last month. 'The one with the disgusting crewcut with matching overalls and big clumpy boots,' she adds. She then asks, somewhat huskily, if I'd like to come over for dinner tonight. Since I suspect it'll be *casserole à la home-grown, hydroponique, organique et revolting*, I turn her down by telling her I've already got five dates, four dinner invitations and three parties to choose from. Get off the phone sick with jealousy at my own elaborate lies. Take a long hot bath and stare at a razor blade with meaning and intent.

*See Tuesday, 6 August.

Sunday   11 August
Legs and underarms now completely hairless, I'm still feeling low, so lie on my bed consumptive-like and read women's magazines for about 15 hours. Am dismayed to learn that research by brainy-stupid people suggests breast-fed babies are more likely to get a date than their bottle-fed peers. Since my cold and heartless mother weaned me on formula, I obviously never stood a chance.

Monday   12 August
Just as my spookily accurate accountant predicted last month, the buzzards at the Inland Revenue have decided to harass me again. They've assured me it's a random audit and has nothing to do with the fact they're envious because I work in advertising and they don't. What I want to know is why they can't pick on dishonest people like all my friends. Thankfully, it's for this year's return which I have not yet lodged; therefore giving me a chance to

readjust my expense claims and be robbed of about two thousand pounds. Ring my convicted number-cruncher and abuse him thoroughly for getting me into this mess in the first place. (When I first hired him through the British Government's rent-a-convict scheme, because he was cheaper than anyone else, he omitted to advise me that, as a notorious embezzler, counterfeiter and money launderer with 32 prior convictions, his clients would be prime targets for investigation by the Inland Revenue.)

Since my accountant's currently sharing a cell with a defrocked Anglican priest who wants to convert him – though not in the biblical sense – my accountant seems happy enough to be verbally berated for over 20 minutes. After I've finally run of breath, he stalls for more time and asks me if I'm still keeping a record of my financial expenses for this fiscal year.

'Yes,' I snap tersely. 'You-can-find-it-on-page-three-in-the-*London-Goss*-lifestyle-section,' I quickly add before hanging up.

Tuesday   **13 August**

My rabid boss has just informed me that the fertiliser commercial I recently recorded has just been pulled by the client who believes country folk might think the man in the ad swears too much. How five 'bloody's' and three 'bugger's' can be offensive to people who stick their hands up livestock for a living is completely beyond me.

To commiserate my loss, drag wallflower child Eliza out to lunch at Zilli's. Wary about going there because the last two times I've ended up with serious post-prandial injuries,* Eliza caringly suggests we eat at a local hospital's canteen so I have less distance to cover to get to a stretcher – which I think is a bit rich coming from she who has spent half her life in the casualty ward whilst assorted boyfriends are attached to life-support machines thanks to the Curse of Namambo. I nonetheless bite my tongue and simply tell her that, since I don't wish to add food poisoning to any

*On first visit, contracted a 24-hour viral infection consisting of a blinding headache, severe nausea and cold sweats. On second visit, fractured my ankle after tripping over a Budvar bottle top near the front entrance (see Worker's Compensation Claim – iii, Thursday, 1 August).

future work-related compensation claims, Zilli's it is.

After well over three bottles of expensive chardonnay, courtesy of the ad agency's Visa card, decide I've had enough of Eliza's psycho babblings about how my chakras are out of whack, so embark on some serious table-hopping.

End up having a semi-intelligible chat with a famous film director with no sense of humour and tell him I can't wait for his latest award-winning film to come out on video so I can watch it. Spend the next 30 minutes being bored to death by a lecture about philistines who refuse to sit in cinemas purely because they're all smoke-free zones. Mercifully, Mrs Famous-Film-Director shows up and I tactfully take my leave because I understand the insecurities of second wives who meet their future husband when he was still married to his first one.

Wednesday   **14 August**
Today, I come home to a deluge of fan mail. It's from a secret admirer of my *London Goss* column. His latest offering espouses handy hints to women who can't get a man. Will photocopy it at work tomorrow and circulate it to my female colleagues who are, no doubt, just panting for relationship tips from men who can't get a shag.

Thursday   **15 August**
This morning at work, my fickle editor at *London Goss* begs me to stop writing about the rich, the infamous and the totally pissed off, as his tabloid is now faced with no less than six writs from high places. Stop myself just in time from telling him that there should only be five because I made one of them up. (I'll be interested to see who comes forward to deny they like frolicking with ferrets.)

Friday   **16 August**
Permanently penurious Teddington rings me today at work. He's obviously forgiven me for stealing his 'big break' at *London Goss* because he's calling to invite me over tonight for a boil-in-the-bag dinner with him and his muse at their new hovel in Kentish Town.

I refuse because couples make me feel inadequate – which I'm sure they do deliberately because they're jealous of my exciting, action-packed single girl's life. Spend evening doing tax return.

Saturday   17 August
Finally bored to tears with rebalancing my books, have at last acquiesced to an invitation to dinner at Teddington's unrenovated warehouse. Personally, I wouldn't squat in the place, let alone rent it.

Whilst Teddington's mistrustful muse casts me a baleful look for refusing to eat the M&S chocolate fudge cake Teddington has scrimped and scraped his entire life's savings to purchase especially for me, I entertain them both with amusing little stories about how I'm a massively successful published columnist and Teddington's not.

As usual, Teddington manages to work the conversation back to himself and asks if I can use my direct line to the *London Goss* editor to get him some work. Appalled at the thought of being directly responsible for foisting Teddington's unremitting garbage on *London Goss* readers, I tell him I'll give it my best shot, though I can't make any promises as, unlike Teddington, my editor is a very busy and important man.

Sunday   18 August
Today I have an extremely frustrating lunch with old Phoebe at Café Bohème. She's being far more tight-lipped than usual about her ongoing liaison with someone else's husband. Indeed it takes me a good two minutes to prise any titillating information out of her. And even then, I have to solemnly swear that anything she leaks to me will not wend its way into my *London Goss* column. It seems that Phoebe's deceitful lover is frightened his wife and two daughters will read my public prose and thus catch on to his wicked ways. I must say, I do think he's being unnecessarily paranoid. I'm sure there are heaps of 44-year-old adulterers living in Highgate who sport strawberry-shaped birthmarks on their left upper thigh and own Labradors called 'Horace'.

Get home in early evening and, since I have nothing better to do with my life these days, start pacing my living-room, bedroom, kitchen and bathroom because I've got to draw a home-office floor plan to satisfy the Inland Revenue auditors, who have had the temerity to doubt that I use 85 per cent of my flat for work purposes.

It's a good thing I've got large feet or it would have taken me forever.

Monday   19 August
Wake up with a pain in my left calf. Terrified I've got phlebitis or some other disfiguring disease as my legs are my best asset (so I'm told), detour work and limp poignantly to Doctor Love's. The source of my chronic hypochondria says I've probably pulled a muscle. Tell him this is impossible as I only move excessively during sex and I've been celibate for well over three hours now. Perhaps realising the pressures of such rampant sexual athleticism, Doctor Love prescribes me with another batch of sedatives.

Tuesday   20 August
Sedatives not working. Leg still hurting. Decide to take a well-earned break whilst I convalesce. At work, ring my travel agent and demand to know how far the frequent-flier points I accrued from my return trip to Singapore last month will take me. Am not thrilled to hear 'an upgrade from cattle to economy on a one-way flight to Newcastle' down the phone. Proceed to then pull a few strings with our agency's over-55's retirement-fund client. Tell him if he wants his annual report written on time this year, I'll have to get into the 'mind-set' of the consumer. Was hoping he'd bankroll a holiday in Miami but end up with a free cruise/fly trip to Ireland.

Wednesday   21 August
My depressed state must be making me uncommonly unbearable because my boss signs my holiday application form willingly – despite the fact this means he will have to do some work for a

change. Take the rest of the day off to pack one pair of jeans, two jumpers and three large boxes of prophylactics.

Thursday   22 August

Spend god-awful night on floating carpark-from-hell in Irish Sea. Cannot sleep because a) I feel seasick and b) in the cabin next to me the two shrinking violets with limited vocabulary ('harder, harder' and 'yes, yes') are keeping me awake.

Get up instead and prowl the corridors in my fetching new PJs in the hope of meeting some lone male tourist who's also looking for the love of his life on a boat headed for Dublin. Arrive in the main lounge area which has been commandeered by a gaggle of public schoolgirls ecstatic at the thought of slumming it west of Sloane Square. Deciding they might make good research material for when I get really desperate and have to write articles for *More!* for a living, I join them. Like all good, well brought-up Protestant types, they attempt to drink me under the table – but it takes more than three bottles of Absolut to make me buckle.

Friday   23 August

Herded off boat at Dublin a complete wreck and collapse on to bed at B&B, shunning the communal breakfast, despite disappointed looks from my hovering hosts. Wake up hours later, notice it's still light, so go back to sleep again. I must be suffering from jet lag. In late afternoon, cab it down to Cork. The roads are quiet, the countryside is endless and I can see why old people flock here.

Many tedious hours and a surprisingly large fare later, arrive at luxury retreat. Too tired to go out so watch in-house movie about a slightly unhinged but brilliant musician who I once met in the Kimberleys in Western Australia when I wrote travel reports for a living. Not knowing who he was and, mistaking him for one of the locals, I nostalgically remember us having a brief but poignant tussle over my bag of lollies outside a motor inn. Fortunately, my host and head of an Australian airline carrier rushed to my side and whispered things like: 'world famous, a bit eccentric' and 'for

God's sake, let go of his bloody fingers', thereby saving Mr Candy Thief from never playing the piano again.

Must admit am a trifle miffed our compelling little scene in the outback didn't make it on to the small screen.

Saturday 24 August

Don't get up late enough to miss hotel's complimentary bus tour of Cork. Faced with about two dozen wrinklies, one of whose colostomy bags I could swear is leaking, I sneak off at the first toilet stop – which just so happens to be in the town centre. Try a bit of civilised clothes shopping but after about the twentieth woolly jumper store, leg it back to lodge.

By nightfall, am feeling incredibly homesick so phone all my friends on the mainland. None of them are in, of course, since London has things called 'pubs' and 'clubs' and 'good times had by all'. Leave reproachful but non-malevolent messages on everyone's answering machines.

Sunday 25 August

Realising I've probably clocked up a huge overseas phone bill – as well as a rather hefty room service tab – go to reception first thing in the morning and tell the old man at the desk I wish to see some sights. Spend at least half an hour pretending to genuinely admire the historic landmarks in the brochures he's given me. Then, when I've lulled him into a false sense of security and he's tottered off to attend to another guest's bedpan, reach behind the counter, steal my credit card imprint, duck outside, flag down cab, end up at Dublin airport, smile winningly at gay check-in officer and immediately get upgraded to first class (which just goes to show I haven't lost my touch). On my way to the plane, handsome steward offers to carry my hand luggage for me. Without thinking, I tell him, thanks, but I'm a feminist, instantly and irrevocably blowing my chances of renewing my subscription to the mile-high club.

While away extremely short flight by scribbling out postcards to my London friends. Drop them in postbox at Heathrow on landing.

Monday   **26 August**
                                                   Bank Holiday
Spend exciting first day back in London unpacking
complimentary soaps, shower caps, emery boards, shoe polish,
shampoos, conditioners, bath oils, tea bags, coffee, sugar, and
cheese and biscuits purloined from my room in Cork. That's what
I like about staying in hotels – I don't have to go grocery shopping
for at least a week afterwards.

Tuesday   **27 August**
My 17-year-old sister Carlotta lands on my doorstep at nine o'clock
in the morning, having just travelled all the way from Barnsley
where she usually lives with my parents.

This is a bit embarrassing as I don't remember inviting her over.
(When asking for favours, my cunning mother likes to corner me
on the phone late at night when I am full of artificially derived
bonhomie followed by inevitable blackout.) As soon as I've thrown
Carlotta into the shower, make like I'm prepared for her much-
anticipated visit by kicking dirty clothes under the bed and
chucking three chocolates on her pillow, along with note saying,
'Don't steal the towels'. Realising there's not enough time to help
her get rid of her northern accent, point her in the direction of
Knightsbridge and tell her that she's got eight hours to develop
some dress sense.

Arrive back at work only to discover my boss is furious that I
took holidays without his consent. Apparently he thought he was
signing my resignation form. He's also none too pleased about the
fact that when he had to write my ads for me, he discovered his
laptop was missing. Faced with a particularly accusatory look, I
think quickly on my feet and do what everyone else does in our
agency when something goes missing, and blame it on the
cleaners.

Afterwards, start frantically ringing my friends in order to
organise a gruelling social whirlwind tour for Carlotta. Sadly for
me, all of them remember her last fateful visit. Even ever-reliable
Eliza begs off, saying she's washing her hair all week, which I can

believe, given the state it's in. Indeed, the only person willing to rally round and help me out is my green-thumbed friend Sophie. She eagerly invites me over for dinner on Thursday though I, of course, failed to mention I'll be bringing a guest.

Carlotta drops by the agency in late afternoon laden down with bags from shops I wouldn't be seen dead in. Proceed to whisk her off to a Soho bar in order that she learn a thing or two from the turtle-necked Turks of London. However, this doesn't cut it with Carlotta who's deliberately worn a tie-dye T-shirt in public to humiliate me. Time stands still as extras from the *Melrose Place* funeral scene spot the sole cast member from *Hair*. The place would have folded right then and there had I not whipped a tablecloth off the nearest table and thrown it over my sister.

Wednesday   28 August
Take Carlotta into work today because I don't trust her when she is out of my sights. Of course, since I refuse to let her anywhere near my own office for fear work colleagues might think we're related, I park her on the eighteenth-century chaise longue in the foyer so she and the Gatekeeper can scowl at each other for the next six and a half hours. Within minutes, the Gatekeeper buzzes my extension and, in scandalised tones, informs me that my errant sibling is necking with a young motorcycle courier. This is all I need. Word will be round the industry in no time: *Katya Livingston's sister necks with illiterates.* Carlotta comfortingly reassures me it was just a meaningless fling and says she's actually going through an older man phase at the moment.

Help her get over it by taking her to the Sad and Over-40's Night at the Atlantic Bar. Wait the prerequisite one and a half minutes it takes for ponytailed geriatrics to hobble over and ply us with copious amounts of drink – then tell the lot of them they're a bunch of hopeless old has-beens who should never have left their wives.

Thursday   29 August
Miss work altogether today thanks to Carlotta encouraging me to have a nightcap comprising of the cheap moonshine she's taken to

distilling in an effort to subsidise her student loan. In fact, Carlotta and I only manage to get up in time for dinner at Sophie's place in Muswell Hill.

My pal of the other persuasion seems slightly disappointed at seeing my little sibling trailing behind me. She starts doing odd things like switching on the overheads, snuffing out the candles, and throwing an Aran cardie over her low-cut flannelette nightie, before eventually putting out another place setting on the cosy table for two.

Not used to cordon bleu cooking of any kind, and especially not the oyster, the truffle or the lobster variety, Carlotta proceeds to spit everything out onto her side plate whilst I look on in mute horror. Sophie appears a little tense and drawn too, especially when Carlotta starts snacking on the home-grown tulips from the floral centrepiece.

Friday   **30 August**
Sophie leaves a message on my answering machine early this morning, saying she read somewhere that tulip bulbs are deadly poisonous. This could be wishful thinking on her part but I don't like to take any chances. Grab the emergency stomach pump from my kitchen drawer and race to the guest room. Carlotta wakes up gagging and gasping whilst I'm busily inserting the tube into her mouth. She assures me she's fine as she only ate three petals.

Go to work but too distraught to do anything.

By evening, feel slightly better so go to Zilli's because Carlotta wants to hone the skills I taught her on Wednesday night. In a cruel twist of fate, her first two subjects just happen to be major advertising bigwigs who could be the difference between a £50,000 and a £150,000 salary for me in the future. Meal Ticket No. 1 looks like Prince on stilts and is wearing an interesting faux-mink coat. He takes a fancy to my sister and she takes my lessons in unarmed combat a tad too far. A flurry of fur and a 'Get lost, wanker' and it's all over in seconds. Meal Ticket No. 2 saves the day and any further career devastation on my part by kindly offering to drop me and Carlotta home. Given that my sister is six-foot tall and filled to the top with Southern Comfort, I almost need the jaws of life to extract her from the back seat of his Porsche.

Saturday   31 August

After much air-kissing and promises about how we must do this all again some time soon, hustle a humungously hung over Carlotta into a station-bound cab and send her back to her natural habitat. In evening, whilst writing out no less than 23 apology notes, my mother calls to tick me off for corrupting my little sister. Apparently she had to be raced off to a Seventh Day Adventist's health farm the minute she disembarked in Barnsley and is now being treated for malnutrition and alcohol poisoning as a direct result of visiting me. I sharply retort that the bad habits Hurricane Carlotta picked up from London are nothing compared to the irreparable damage she managed to inflict upon my career and social life during her short stay.

Sunday   1 September

It seems I'm being put upon by yet another person who can't handle their alcohol. Whilst finishing itemising almost every penny I earned last financial year in order to keep tax jackals at bay, I receive a phone call from my boss. Fortunately, it turns out he's not ringing to impinge on my leisure time but to request that I look after a couple of minor details tomorrow because he's going into hospital to get his liver drained.

Monday   2 September

Waste entire morning traipsing around some suburban shopping centre looking for clothes for the Gatekeeper, the 'star' of a furniture commercial I'm overseeing this week on behalf of my boss. The old soak refuses to fork out for paid professionals to appear in our telly commercials, claiming he can't be expected to pay my salary and Equity rates as well. He's also too mean to hire a professional stylist. Since being personal dresser to a 40-something *hausfrau* who doesn't wear any colour or fabric particularly well is not part of my job description, am determined to make sure it never happens again.The shop assistant at Miss Selfridges seemed slightly taken aback at my choice of attire for a middle-aged size 16 woman but, under threat of losing a much-needed sale, she wisely keeps her opinions to herself.

Spirits buoyed by my wily purchases, decide to go and spoil it all by grabbing a spot of lunch in what can only loosely be described as the food hall. Proceed to get cornered by socially disadvantaged toddler who makes huge eyes at my 'gourmet' muffin. Reluctantly relenting, thrust my weevil-ridden rock cake into his grubby paws and then make a dash for the carpark before he starts gagging over his mother's flip-flops.

Arrive back at ad agency and then have to leave again because my *London Goss* editor has left a message to say he wants to see me urgently – no doubt to give me a well-earned pay rise.

Tuesday   3 September
Having just been ordered to get a sex life by my depraved tabloid editor in an effort to boost my readership ratings and salary alike, spend good part of working day frantically rubbing the pink love crystal Eliza gave me in Glastonbury. So far, the stupid thing hasn't worked – unless you count the window cleaner who winked at me outside my office window this morning – but I daren't chuck it out. Just in case.

Wednesday   4 September
Continue my quest for more money and sexual respect over lunch at Café Bohème with Phoebe and Ferguson. Normally I don't allow my individual friends to socialise with each other in case they start bitching about me behind my back, but with Phoebe and Ferguson I'm willing to make an exception to the rule. Since they've got so much in common (penchant for falling in love with married men, tendency to wear far too much eyeliner, etcetera, etcetera), I'm hoping they'll dump on each other for a change and take the pressure off me.

Whilst they swap relationship techniques and make-up tips, I lean over the menu so the waiter can see my cleavage which is fairly impressive at the best of times. Lick my lips lasciviously while ordering rare beef, suck Bloody Mary suggestively through straw and then chomp on stick of celery in wildly seductive manner. Phoebe tells me I'm overdoing it. Ferguson, who is cringing in the corner, says I'm being a bit obvious. But what would they know? They don't have the pressure of pleasing thousands of readers who have nothing better to do than live their lives vicariously through me. Needless to say, waiter is hopelessly besotted and loiters with intent and obscenely large pepper grinder. I, on the other hand, refuse to acknowledge his desperate signals as I don't go out with men who earn less than me.

Thursday   **5 September**
Today, I'm being forced to bus it to work because I've ran out of company cab vouchers and my skinflint boss refuses to buy me a company car. Mercifully, my bus dodders down the more well-heeled roads of London so it's full of well-dressed people. Indeed, I count only two civil servants.

Deciding to make the best of a bad situation, continue my ongoing manhunt whilst in transit. As the bus lurches to a start, proceed to launch myself into a nearby businessman's lap. Cunning plan foiled mid-air by some interfering conductor who puts out an unhelpful hand and then guides me to an empty seat three rows further down. I reward him with a falsely appreciative smile through 32 gritted teeth and no doubt make his day even though he's managed to completely wreck mine.

Not in fabulously brilliant mood when I arrive at agency to catch the Gatekeeper struggling to read a postcard. Instinctively knowing it must be addressed to me because I'm the only person in the agency who has jetsetting friends, I snatch it from her. It's from Sabelo, my African tax loss. With only 39 spelling mistakes and 14 grammatical errors to his credit, he declares that when he's not busy begging for food he likes to fashion miniature cars out of scrap metal and sell them on the roadside to witless Western tourists.

To cut a short, barely comprehensible story even shorter, he's writing to ask me if Great Britain is a potential export market.

And, if so, would I consider acting as his overseas agent? Half-tempted to commission him on behalf of those Portobello Road boutiques that insist upon selling ugly *objets d'art*. Contrary to his charity organisation's claims, however, I do not wish to corrupt Sabelo. Poverty-stricken people are usually quite humble, and therefore a lot more endearing than the high-income-tax-bracket sell-outs I'm surrounded by. Write firm but friendly letter back to Sabelo telling him he can't be expected to rely on the kindness of overseas strangers all the time. Advise him to lower his sights a little and concentrate on more modest business ventures closer to home. To let him down gently, enclose *How to Succeed in a Cottage Industry* which my boss recently purchased because he's finding it hard to meet office lease payments.

Friday   **6 September**
Spend all day with handsome cinematographer who has a dreadfully annoying speech impediment. Probably could have scored a date if I hadn't pointed this fact out to him. Also come to blows with him over my choice of clothes for the Gatekeeper's debut TV appearance. He thinks the latex rubber skirt and leopard-print halter is a little over the top for someone flogging furniture. I just tell him to stop stuttering and get on with the job at hand. Needless to say, the Gatekeeper seems to like all the attention she's getting. Not realising that film crews are paid to flatter the talent, at the end of the shoot she asks me if she can keep the clothes. I let her, of course – but only because they're three sizes too big for me.

At end of day, head off to Teddington and his muse's house-warming at their unrenovated Kentish Town warehouse. Upon arrival, pick my way delicately around orange-boxes posing as tables and bean bags pretending to be chairs and toss a gift-wrapped ashtray at the happy hovel-dwellers (they're both heavy smokers). Teddington asks if I've managed to put in a good word for him to my editor at *London Goss*. Since it's completely slipped my mind to help lower the tone of this city's leading tabloid by one fell swoop of Teddington's pen, I lie and say I spoke to my editor at length and he suggested Teddington try submitting his work to the *Evening Standard* first. Ignoring the furious glare from his nearby muse, I then join the heaving throng of well-wishers, all of whom appear to be struggling in their search for an identity. One of the more successful ones has green dreadlocks and what looks like a spanner through his nose. Soon get rid of him off by telling him I work in advertising and like to harpoon whales on my days off.

Saturday   **7 September**
Tonight, Eliza's having her undisclosed age birthday party at a tapas bar in Soho. At the very last minute, ring her and say I can't come because, much as I value her friendship, I'm a vixen with a deadline to meet and I'm hardly likely to meet it surrounded by all her boring old spinster friends. Resolve weakens somewhat when Eliza tells me that the single men there will outnumber the single women by three to one. Speed over to tapas bar and casually plonk myself between the eligible trio. Then proceed to stun them with my inherent wit, beauty and intelligence. One is old enough to be my father but keeps buying me tequilas (sucker). One has a really nice personality and buys me a rose (loser). The other is a dark and handsome Italian who tries to ignore me (bastard). Call me shallow, but Bastard it is. We salsa, I swoon and he tries to put his arms around me. Then he tells me his girlfriend has just left him – no doubt expecting a little horizontal sympathy from me. Sadly for him, I don't mate with men who can't hold a relationship together. Proceed to get plastered and catch a minicab home alone. Invite driver up for coffee but don't think he understands, English being his second language.

Sunday   **8 September**
Get up at about two in the afternoon feeling distinctly unwell. Eliza rings to say she's going to Petticoat Lane with Loser and Sucker as they've now latched on to her since they can't have me. Pretend to be put out in order to boost her self-esteem. Am sincerely hoping Loser and Sucker don't come to too much grief

for I was too busy with Bastard last night to think to warn them about the Curse of Namambo.

In evening, still feel unwell but head for the Night Cat anyway because I'm meeting with Sophie for drinks. (Thankfully, she appears to have forgiven me for my sibling's atrocious behaviour at her place last month). Over several hairs of the dog with Sophie, and whilst taking deliberate care to ignore the barman who is looking at me with obvious intent, I bemoan my loveless plight. After a few slugs of Jack Daniels, Sophie runs a calloused hand through her short spiky crop and says quite coyly for a woman who's built like a tractor, that she can think of at least one person who'd like to sleep with me. This might be so, I reply, casting another lingering glance at the broad back of the barman who has now moved on to stage two of universal pick-up rituals, but I don't like being seen with men who pull pints for a living.

Monday   **9 September**
Arrive at ad agency, only to have the Gatekeeper excitedly inform me that Eliza has taken the day off work because she is visiting a couple of friends in hospital. What's more, says the Gatekeeper, there's a 'surprise' waiting for me in my office. My horror is of truly titanic proportions when I find a small, skinny, bespectacled thing sitting at Suzette's old desk. March straight to my boss, who is now back from the dead, drag away the brandy that's about to touch his convalescing lips and demand to know what that thing with bad teeth and a crayon in his hand is doing sharing an office with me. Boss tightly informs me that since the agency desperately needs an art director and since no one employable will work with me, he's had to bring in a work-experience student. What's more, he says, since young Sebastian is a novice, it is my duty to guide him.

Stumble straight to the café next door and ask for a packet of Panadol. The acne-riddled apprentice chef there gives me a Lucozade on the house, telling me I look like I need it. I must say – and I did – this is very rich coming from someone who could best be described as 'massively unattractive' even on a good day.

Tuesday   **10 September**

Eliza arrives back at work today. Apparently Loser and Sucker narrowly escaped death when some shop-front scaffolding collapsed on top of them. Both are progressing well at a reputable rehabilitation centre and are soon expected to be able to eat their own meals without assistance or bibs.

A little more pale and drawn than usual, Eliza nonetheless willingly lets me raid the agency's employee work files so I can confirm that Sebastian is indeed being paid standard work experience rates. Finally satisfied he's earning £50,000 less than me (i.e. nothing), Eliza and I then go to the café next door to grab some lunch. Come back with an additional custard tart, compliments of the apprentice chef who seems to get off on wholesale abuse for putting Cheddar instead of Swiss in my chicken escalope sandwich.

Eliza, the brain surgeon, reckons I've got an admirer.

Wednesday   **11 September**

My boss is on the rampage again. He's just seen the telly commercial starring the Gatekeeper and gives me a monumental dressing-down, yelling that: '*No one in their right mind would buy a Chesterfield from someone who looks like a total trollop.*'

Of course, Total Trollop just happens to be eavesdropping behind my office door at the time in full rubber rig-out and promptly bursts into tears before racing off to the ladies. Fed up with all the high theatrics that seem to constantly engulf me, I retreat to the café next door for some peace and quiet. The apprentice chef and I make polite chit-chat about how to make a latte properly. Three hours later, and having finally had his fill of vicious insults for the day, he then asks if I'd like to meet for drinks at TGI Fridays. I graciously refuse, adding I don't go anywhere that's got a happy hour, nor do I wish to fraternise with the typing pool. Get back to work only to discover that, in my absence, Sebastian has been trying to write good ads by himself in a sad and pathetic attempt to usurp my position as most valuable and therefore most highly paid employee.

Set him straight immediately by putting all his ads in the bin.

Thursday   12 September

Still no luck on the mating front, so decide to do what most of the men in this industry do, and abuse my position of power. After flicking through the mug shots in a national casting directory, order the ravishing Reef (pronounced Rolf) for a new radio ad which is being recorded this afternoon, well ahead of schedule and well before my boss gets to read the script. Whilst I think it's my best work to date, I suspect that old Yellow Liver will baulk at using such a brave and potentially headline-hitting concept to sell life assurance. Reef seems a bit surprised at being cast as a middle-aged housewife, particularly one who's planning to murder her husband for monetary gain. Nevertheless, he acts suitably grateful for the work, and for the opportunity to eye me up as I lie languidly on a strategically positioned couch.

Much to the consternation of the sound engineer, I chuck a Stanley Kubrick and make my quarry do a record 738 takes. Then, still not completely satisfied I've made my romantic intentions clear enough, toss Reef a Fisherman's Friend and tell him to come back tomorrow.

When I arrive back at the agency to collect my phone messages at five in the evening, am not amused to see Sebastian still hard at work even though it is now officially after hours. He's obviously trying to earn brownie points with management but he's wasting his time. Our boss has fallen off the wagon and into Oddbins, so wouldn't have a clue that Sebastian's being so conscientious. And, as the wheedling little worm's mentor, I'm certainly not going to help him wiggle up the food chain.

Friday   13 September

Receive an exceptionally disturbing phone call from Reef's agent today. She says that thanks to my exacting demands, her charge has developed throat nodules and will now only be able to audition for non-speaking roles in the future. Since I refuse to consort with extras, nor indeed mime artists, this means I am back to square one. Realising at this rate I'll never get my pay rise from *London Goss*, decide to take some fairly drastic measures. Clearly not used to an attractive women making a lunge for him over the basins in the men's loo, Sebastian querulously informs me he's already got a girlfriend. Stuck for any better excuses, he then says he doesn't fancy me. This I find extremely hard to believe. But, if Sebastian wants to live in a state of constant denial, then so be it. To show there are no hard feelings, go into our mutual office, accidentally break his favourite coffee mug, mistakenly scribble over his Louise poster and carelessly remove all the lids from his felt-tip pens.

Then spend fruitless evening at supermarket as 'reliable source' Eliza tells me this is where all the eligible men hang out. Tonight, however, the ones *sans* two heads certainly aren't stocking up on Lean Cuisine at Sainsburys.

Saturday   **14 September**
Don't go out in the evening. Instead, start plotting the second and last stage of my sex-for-pay offensive.

Sunday   **15 September**
More bothersome birthday bashes. This time it's Ferguson's turn to try and scam a gift from a hard-up friend who hasn't bought him one. He's holding his acquisitive outing at Freedom in Soho. Steel myself for the inevitable wrist flapping and catty comments from all his fairy friends. However, specially for me, Ferguson has made sure there are at least some men present who like women. Drag the least ugly and most famous one home for coffee and refills. For legal reasons, cannot divulge who he is or what we did. However, all will be revealed very soon in a well-paying women's weekly under the headline: YOUNG BEAUTY SAYS MR STUD WAS DUD!!!

Monday   **16 September**
Wake up with chronic bronchitis. He-whose-name-cannot-be-mentioned-if-I-want-my-hard-earned-ten-grand-and-Honda-Civic-

hatchback-from-a-leading-women's-magazine must have given it to me (no pun intended). Wish I hadn't sent him packing at three o'clock this morning because at least now I could start making him feel adequate and useful by sending him off to the shops to pick up some cough mixture.

Soldier on into work to milk my illness for all it's worth. Line up copious amounts of pills and potions along my desk. Wrap one of the agency's Persian rugs around my shoulders. Then wilfully cough and splutter all over Sebastian, my boss and a very important small-goods client. Needless to say, I'm sent home just in time to catch Doctor Love before he finishes his shift* at the surgery. Am fairly flattered to see that he's now so in tune with my outwardly perfect but inwardly ailing body, he can automatically hand me a prescription before I've even told him what's wrong.

*Mon to Wed 9 a.m.–1 p.m., Thur to Fri 8 a.m.–5 p.m., Sat 9 a.m.–3 p.m.

Tuesday   **17 September**
Sedatives not helping flu much, so ring Phoebe every ten minutes for about two hours until she finally comes round to play nursemaid. Whilst I croak orders from my bed, she cheers me up with more stories about her sad and doomed life – including the one about how she's so sick of being a kept woman, she's decided to assert her independence by taking on lousy paying reception work at the escort agency where Ferguson works. (This is the result of doing a good deed and letting two no-hoper friends get their heads together.) I facetiously suggest she try crossing the counter in order to supplement her meagre income. Phoebe replies, in all sincerity, that she can't bring herself to cheat on her married lover.

Wednesday   **18 September**
Still too ill to go to work today. For medicinal purposes only, cab it over to West End to cadge free drinks off the junior barman at the Coach & Horses. As usual, Teddington is behind the bar staring disconsolately at a dish towel instead of serving his non-paying customers. After he's poured me a carafe of fine Chablis, he asks me not to write about him any more in my *London Goss* column as his

muse is getting very upset. Not only that, she's actually threatening to leave him because he's becoming such a social embarrassment. And, adds Teddington, his voice quivering petulantly, if she does leave him, he may be forced to throw himself off the Oxo Tower.

Sick of being every bleeding heart's scapegoat, particularly when I'm so unwell, I bang my empty carafe on the counter and crossly tell Teddington that I wish he hadn't told me this since I don't need any more encouragement to publicly vilify his literary talents.

Thursday   **19 September**
Arrive back at work and make a demented dash for the office mail before the Gatekeeper gets her thieving hands on the free women's magazines our agency regularly receives from genuflecting sales reps. Grab the one that features my sordid exposé on Mr Stud, leave agency and head straight over to *London Goss* headquarters. After showing my editor the printed proof of my first-ever sexual liaison since my column started (and subsequently extracting the financial equivalent of six bottles of Christian Dior Joy parfum per week), arrive back at the ad agency to find Sebastian the Grave Robber rifling through a case of award-winning wines (which were a present for me from a grateful vineyard client before he realised I'd been faking it). Sebastian's look of horror at seeing me alive and well more than makes up for his petty pilfering.

Friday   **20 September**
No doubt inspired by my self-administered dose of publicity in a leading women's glossy yesterday, the head of non-fiction at a Scottish independent publishing house rings today and asks if I'd be interested in writing a tell-all book about my one-night stand with Mr Stud. Since there's not an awful lot to tell, I say I'd be happy to pen a slim volume for her. Determined not to be ripped off by money-grubbing book 'binders', decide I'd better find myself a literary agent, so she can rip me off instead. Steal the Yellow Pages from reception when the Gatekeeper's not looking and start to phone around.

First off the list is Agents With Attitudes, one of whom superciliously informs me she only deals with dead poets and living legends. Just as I'm about to argue my case, my boss interrupts and orders me to accompany Sebastian to an advertising function at Soho House because Sebastian is too scared to go to trendy places by himself for fear the in-crowd catch on to the fact he's a sad case with no real friends. As a reward for my good deed, I make Sebastian introduce me to SpaceBoy, an old acquaintance of his. SpaceBoy is good-looking in a weird kind of way and stares at me with flattering intensity whilst I get completely rat-faced on the drinks he buys me and insult him with customary flair and vigour. As usual, my feminine wiles work a treat and he asks me for my phone number.

Saturday   **21 September**
Spend all morning with my ear pressed to my answering machine, screening calls so that when SpaceBoy rings I can pretend I'm out. By late afternoon, he's obviously still plucking up the courage to call, so take the phone off the hook to thwart his efforts further. Then, in a fit of ill temper and therefore extremely bad judgement, stomp off to Teddington's to have a good moan. Typically, I'm outdone by him whingeing about insensitive judges who chose not to include him in the Granta Best of Young British Novelists issue this year. I tactfully change the subject by waxing lyrically for hours upon end about my fabulously successful column and my pending book contract.

Depart soon after, leaving Teddington a broken and shattered man and, still as yet, an unpublished writer.

Sunday   **22 September**
Reconnect phone. No word from SpaceWimp.

Monday   **23 September**
It seems that totally crap female impersonator Reef has managed to get me into some serious trouble. Indeed, our agency has just lost its biggest account because the life-assurance client said that

the homicidal housewife in his new ad sounds 'a bit like a bloke'. To make matters worse, catch Sebastian, the clot, spilling coffee over my computer in yet another clumsy attempt to short-circuit my career. Teach him a lesson from the best by dobbing him and his prolific Glu-Stick habit in to our accounts department.

Still no word from SpacePig.

Tuesday   **24 September**

Today, whilst trying to do some work at the agency, Calliope, soon-to-be seamstress to the stars, calls me to say she's now in Rome running up Shroud of Turin knock-offs for a tablecloth merchant and has just had her genitals pierced. By what? I innocently ask. Calliope guffaws down the line, coyly adding that it's supposed to do wonders for a girl's sex life. Resolve to get mine done also – that is, until the Gatekeeper, who as usual heard everything, informs me in hushed tones that she's heard that it enhances men's pleasure too. That does it. Men get enough orgiastic delight from me without being encouraged.

Wednesday   **25 September**

At precisely 11:07:33, trying valiantly not to sound like he hasn't been counting the hours and minutes and seconds to hear my voice, SpaceBoy rings to ask me out for lunch. Play hard to get and say no, but how about dinner? In a petty attempt at power play, he says no, but how about tomorrow evening? Tempted to tell him I'm douching but after second thoughts don't. Strangely enough, Sebastian appears delighted by the turn of events. He even adds that SpaceBoy and I are very well-suited.

Thursday   **26 September**

Spend best part of the morning charging round Knightsbridge in order to purchase a drop-dead gorgeous but not too try-hard frock for my big date tonight. Then take the rest of the day off to attend to my hair, nails and make-up. When I'm positive I look like the wife of Croesus after her divorce settlement comes through, slink into Dome on King's Road and prepare to connect with SpaceBoy.

I must say, I feel a real meeting of the minds when he grandly informs me that he is a certified Satanist. I'm further impressed when he tells me in a conspiratorial whisper that the salt cellars at the next table have been following him all evening. But have to draw the line when he asks the waiter for some water and starts shovelling down lithium tablets at the dinner table. Promptly ask for the bill, give it to SpaceCadet, then bolt for the door.

Sebastian is going to pay for this big time tomorrow.

Friday   27 September

Creep into ad agency through the fire exit so no one will spot me and therefore ask how the psycho-sideshow that was my date with SpaceBoy went. Upon spying me writing ads from under my desk, Sebastian, with typical malicious intent, pops the question straight away. I curtly reply that my coupling went as well as could be expected when one of us has debilitating mental problems.

Predictably, SpaceBoy calls me later on, no doubt to apologise profusely for his atrocious behaviour last night. Fortunately, I'd already had the good sense to instruct the Gatekeeper (whose job it is to screen my suitors and field my social calls) to issue the standard party line and tell him I was tragically killed in a freak accident during the shooting of a TV commercial today. Indeed, the entire agency is currently in mourning and is closing down for a week. SpaceTwit believes her and asks when the burial is taking place, no doubt intending to throw himself into my grave for a bit of a forage. Gatekeeper is then forced to drastically improvise and says it's by private invitation only, adding (in unnecessarily sarcastic tones, I think) that the deceased does not as yet qualify for a state funeral.

Saturday   28 September

Start feeling insecure about my looks since they only appear to attract halfwits, so get my eyelashes permed. Then, in evening, go clubbing by myself at Café de Paris and bat them ferociously at every man in sight, losing a contact lens in the process. I must say, the place doesn't look half as flash with all the lights on and two hundred male patrons scrabbling about on the floor looking for a piece of semi-permeable plastic.

Sunday   29 September

Eliza rings to invite me to go to Camden Market. I politely decline because stepping over syringes and trying to avoid the local colour is not my idea of a good time. Also, I'm terrified I'll bump into SpaceBoy. The last thing I need is for him to have a turn when he spots my corpse swanning around London.

Monday   30 September

Still looking for a stupid literary agent for my as-yet unwritten tell-all tome. Have only made my way through to 'S' for 'Snooty Sales People' in the Yellow Pages. Upon hearing a brief outline of my illustrious career to date, the receptionist there refuses to put my call through, saying the company doesn't handle trashy books, nor indeed, authors. This sends me into fits of depression, causing me to eat all of Sebastian's Milky Ways which he has stupidly tried to hide from me by taping them to the underneath of his desk. Ensuing sugar-high plummets when a wreath arrives at agency. It's from SpaceBoy. 'Dear Katya,' he's written on the card in what looks awfully like human haemoglobin. 'Until we meet again at the other side.' Over my dead body, I grimly think, as I wrestle half a tonne of lilies into a vase.

Tuesday   1 October

Me and Sebastian's relationship plunges to new depths at work today after I catch him trying to slip full-cream milk into my coffee when he knows perfectly well I only take skimmed. Hurl plunger and milk jug at him in a singularly spectacular fashion and soon have him cowering in the corner. Then, just as I've got a fork poised ready to deliver the final *coup de grâce*, my boss staggers into the kitchen for his mid-morning tipple. Upon seeing me wild-eyed and hair askew, he starts to back out again. Down cutlery and follow him to his office, all the while yelling about how, since I've just decided to quit smoking, I can no longer tolerate working with an underhanded, untalented creep like Sebastian – and can he be sacked, please? Boss sighs long and heavily, deems this impossible and then reluctantly reveals what I have long suspected: Sebastian is the nephew of one of our more profitable clients. I caustically reply it seems strange that Uncle Client would wittingly sabotage his ads by insisting Sebastian work on them.

Wednesday   2 October
Spend morning at work chomping furiously on nicotine gum. This is because, in future, I do not wish to be unfairly accused of causing fire hazards in the fire-exit stairwell. (A vindictive office cleaner recently complained to management about the mountains of cigarette butts he spied there and Sebastian the Lion-Heart blamed it all on me though, later on, and armed with tweezers and dustpan and brush, I did manage to prove a point by separating Seb's staggering 1,537 Benson & Hedges Extra-Mild dog-ends from my measly 1,082 Marlboro Reds.)

Naturally, I'm not in the best of moods when, during my seemingly never-ending search for an agent for my tell-all tome, some woman at No Sense of Humour Literary Management ('N' in the Yellow Pages) tells me she won't represent material which pokes fun at a man's impotence problems. That's because she didn't have to sleep with him, I think peevishly to myself. The Gatekeeper doesn't help matters when she sticks her head into my office and asks when she can have her stupid phone directories back.

Thursday   3 October
Resort to nicotine patches to quell my cravings. Still manage to consume half my lifetime allowance of calories by eating three bagels, two muesli bars, half a packet of M&Ms, a tangerine and a sausage in batter before lunchtime. Sebastian says I look like I've put on weight. Snarl back at him that at least I didn't get my job through nepotism. The nephew-from-hell immediately runs squalling to my boss who in turn hauls me into his office, muttering something about 'attitude problems'. Why he can't tell Sebastian this himself, I have no idea.

Friday   **4 October**
Today, after throwing Eliza and her acupuncture, hypnotherapy
and raki brochures out of my office, the Gatekeeper comes in and,
rather smugly, hands me a postcard from Africa. In his inimitable,
illegible scrawl, Sabelo begs me for bail money. Apparently, he is
doing time for selling water on the black market from the well I am
financing for him and his family. Instinctively want to tell him off
for being such a selfish, uncaring little brat but nonetheless write
out the requested five-pound cheque because I still have hopes
he'll veer back on to the path of righteousness and become a
basketball player one day, thus supporting me in my dotage.

    Later, in another dismal attempt to help try and keep my mind
off my Marlboros, Eliza takes me to some dazed and confused pub
in the East End. The bouncers are girls, the waitresses are boys and
if you want to eat they order out for pizza. Apparently, they are
being 'ironic'. Like I said to Eliza before flouncing out into the
night, if I wanted to sit in a pigsty and eat takeaway I could have
stayed at home.

Saturday   **5 October**
Start smoking again.

Sunday   **6 October**
Whilst still furiously catching up on five cigarette-free days, Phoebe
rings up with a major personal crisis and pleads with me to fill in
for her overnight at the escort agency switchboard. She suspects
her married lover is sleeping with his wife behind her back so wants
to do a dawn raid on their house in Highgate. Consequently spend
late evening and early morning at a down-at-heel office in Soho
taking phone calls from degenerates. Do my best impersonation of
a tart with a heart by telling the first perverted caller to drop dead.
The next demented soul asks if we do threesomes and, if so, can we
supply a strap-on? A strap-on what? I brusquely bark before
hanging up. Another sad sap confides he 'likes 'em hairy'. Tell him
we don't do hirsute at the Pink Paradise and give the number for
the Hellenic Harlots instead. By the end of the shift, I have saved all

my girls a lot of physical and emotional heartache.

Of course, none of them are the least bit grateful. Instead, they bang on about lost income and hungry sprogs. End up telling them to do what all normal single mothers do and go starve to death in a high-rise council flat.

Monday   7 October
Whilst adding up how many sick-leave days I have left to use up before the end of my working year, Phoebe rings up weeping and wailing and wauling and keening because her lover cruelly dumped her in favour of his wife after the latter issued him with an ultimatum upon seeing Phoebe at the foot of the marital bed. Selflessly rearrange my hectic work schedule and meet old Phoebe for all the juicy goss at Café Bohème. But Phoebe is a completely useless conversation-piece and just sits there looking tragic. I attempt to be a good and loyal friend by saying I never liked him anyway and who really wants to date an overweight, balding adulterer with hairs hanging out of his nostrils?

Strangely, Phoebe just storms off in a huff and leaves me with the bill.

Tuesday   8 October
Much to the relief of the Gatekeeper, I'm sure, have at last secured a literary agent for my current publishing endeavours (found her in the Yellow Pages under 'W', for 'Writers Is Us'). She E-mailed me this morning to say she's 'thrilled and humbled to be working with such a wonderfully talented writer'.

E-mail her back requesting that, in future, she not waste time and paper just to state the patently obvious for there are books to flog and commissions to niggle over.

Wednesday   9 October
Day starts off well when, thanks to the leading women's magazine, my brand-new Honda Civic hatchback arrives along with my cheque for £10,000. Use the former to get me to Harvey Nicks to spend the latter.

Day finishes badly when I get back to work late afternoon and am told by my office informant, Eliza, that my boss has started to pay Sebastian minimum wages because he is 'impressed with his efforts'.

Thursday   **10 October**
Currently on strike over Sebastian's pay conditions.

Friday   **11 October**
Still on strike.

Saturday   **12 October**
Temporarily lift ban on working because I never work weekends anyway.

At lunchtime catch up with my press colleague Sophie at the Globe. She seems enormously pleased to see me and even offers to pay for my meal. Over it, she informs me she's celebrating because she's just come out to her mother and father. Apparently they were 'deeply shocked'. Frankly, I can't see how any parent would think that their daughter was interested in the affections of men when she dresses like Sophie does. It's a wonder *lesbians* give her a second glance. Sophie goes on to say that she's glad she's come clean because it means that she can now take her future girlfriends down to the family farm in Gloucestershire. She pauses and looks at me meaningfully. I look back at her blankly because the thought of some poor, unsuspecting dyke being dragged off to the back of beyond for the weekend doesn't bear thinking about.

In evening, have to sit and suffer through home-made paella at Ferguson's pad in Hampstead because he's still trying to win over his new client, Paolo, who Ferguson swears is more than just a one-hour fling. Whilst I surreptitiously pick bits of still-pulsating sea creatures out from the rice and on to the side of my plate, Paolo tries to impress me with his heritage, saying that he finally realised he was gay after he was savagely gored by a bull in Pamplona. Ferguson just sits by and quietly sulks because, as usual, I'm getting all the attention.

Sunday   13 October

This afternoon when I arrive back home from the chemist's with some Milk of Magnesia to drown the marine life I accidentally swallowed last night, I discover Biggles, my brother, squatting on my doorstep and chewing on a piece of privet hedge. He's been flying crop-sprayers in Senegal for far too long, so his manners are a bit *je ne sais quoi*. Thankfully, he's only paying me a fleeting visit, since he's just in town for the night to drop off five crates of highly illegal African parrots to an unscrupulous and undiscerning trader.

Enormously pleased to see that my brother is now a big-time smuggler as well as a small-time aviator, I reluctantly let him in after first checking the corridor for lurking Customs and Excise officers. Biggles then presents me with a litre of disgusting duty-free bourbon, treats me to dinner at Garfunkels and then, when we get back to my place again, whips out his well-thumbed photo album full of pictures of great-airstrips-he-has-known-in-West-Africa-and-I-have-seen-many-times-before. Try to be patient with him and resist the urge to yawn because – as my mother constantly has to remind me – he is family. Come bedtime, I toss him a rattan mat but Biggles demurs, saying the bathroom floor at the Heathrow Holiday Inn is more to his liking.

Monday   14 October

Go to work to demand a pay rise, only to be told in slightly slurred tones by my permanently pickled employer that he hadn't actually noticed I'd been on strike since I hardly do any work anyway. He also adds that I'd better watch my 'sshtep'. In evening, decide I'd better go to an advertising industry bash at the Dorchester in order to advance my career. Don't get very far as my path is blocked by all the dead wood and dinosaurs from the multi-nationals making a desperate dash to the drinks tray.

Tuesday   15 October

Today, my vindictive boss sends me to Sydenham to meet with a plastic-packaging manufacturer.

On arrival, have a minute's silence for all the people who live there.

Wednesday   **16 October**

Have just found out that whilst I was on strike last week Sebastian the Naïf managed to wreck my clever plan to extract a free island holiday in the Caribbean. (I had almost managed to convince my boss and our continental sausage client that Tobago would be the ideal location for a telly commercial I'm meant to be overseeing next month. Unfortunately, in my absence at the pre-production meeting last Friday, Sebastian the Bigmouth piped up with, 'there's a great little beach down on the Isle of Wight that looks just like Tobago'.)

Thursday   **17 October**

Walk into agency this morning still in high dudgeon, only to discover another one of my boss's outrageously extravagant purchases standing in the foyer. Thanks to his drink-induced short-term memory loss, he's forgotten all about the recent demise of his prized koi and has now decided to risk installing a giant aviary, complete with twittering chaffinches. The noise is appalling – even the Gatekeeper casts them evil looks because they keep constantly interrupting her social calls.

Friday   **18 October**

Current black mood not enhanced today when I find out that my useless agent has omitted to invite me to a literary soirée she's hosting tomorrow night. Indeed, I throw a massive hissy fit, threatening to go public with this appalling oversight when I start the publicity treadmill for my book next year.

My agent back-pedals furiously, promising to strike one of her international visiting authors from the guest list in favour of me.

Saturday   **19 October**

Am stuck in a decrepit house full of threadbare rugs and badly dressed people. Of course, it's my own fault for insisting upon being invited to my agent's idea of a 'party'.

Am thus forced to spend next four hours trying not to choke on stale biscotti all the while enduring young bohemian types who bang on about 'suffering for their art'. I nod meaningfully, pretending I understand what they're saying.

Sunday   20 October
Have to go into work today because it's my turn to ring Calliope.

Make the call from Sebastian's phone since his doesn't yet have a lock on his phone – though I suspect when my boss sees next month's British Telecom bill, it will only be a matter of time.

Calliope is currently in Paris, still trying to make it into prêt-à-porter. She tells me she's met lots of gorgeous young Arabic types who've commissioned her to design blindfolds and yashmaks and a whole host of other exciting things which she says she can't wait to try out.

Monday   21 October
Foolishly taking me at my word, and mistakenly thinking I've actually written my quick-turnaround tell-all tome, my useless agent has just called to say she's secured me a huge advance and has assured my publisher I can deliver the finished manuscript next month. As I took great pains to point out, it's all very well for her to make promises on my behalf, but she doesn't actually have to write the stupid thing from scratch in less than 30 days. Decide I'd better get cracking as of today. Start by organising my author shots. Sebastian says he knows someone who can take a mean snap. Whilst I am loath to take anything on recommendation from Sebastian, he says Tarquin from St Martin's College will take my pictures for free because he's trying to get a portfolio together.

Tuesday   22 October
Get up a couple of minutes earlier than usual because I have to make myself look more ravishing than normal for my photo shoot. In Tarquin's studio/dining-room, I strike seriously sultry, darkly mysterious smoulder. Hands shaking in admiration, Tarquin skols the first of his five morning beers and starts to click away, occasionally asking me to smile a bit more, but which I pretend not to hear because I want my readers to take me seriously.

After three hours of intense pouting, get back to agency thoroughly exhausted. Realising how stressed I am juggling numerous careers at once, Eliza agrees to offer to fetch me my lunch from the café next door. Unfortunately, she brings back a tofu burger because not only is she amazingly plain, she is also stunningly stupid. Furtively feed it to the finches in the foyer.

Wednesday   23 October
My mother rings and, in the sort of hopeful tones I have come to dread, asks me if, now I'm an almost-famous authoress, I've managed to ensnare a boyfriend. Am tempted to tell her that the types of men found sniffing around literary ladies are not the sort I'd be caught dead with under a duvet, let alone alive. But, to keep her happy, tell her I'm being wooed by the devastatingly gorgeous Count Kosciusko from Poland. Get a bit carried away with the whole romantic notion of it all, so add that he's got a whopping great castle in Warsaw and a nice little holiday house in Tuscany which he occasionally sublets to his brother-in-law, the Pope. Now my mother can die content in the knowledge that her daughter's dated minor royalty and I can live in eternal regret for not having gone for broke and nominated a prince instead.

Sadly for me, my small act of kindness badly backfires because bucket-ears Sebastian overhears my conversation and, since he is bereft of a brain and a degree in European Studies, spreads my little fibette round the office. The world of advertising being as it is, within 15 minutes an old acquaintance of mine rings from Rotterdam to commend me upon my latest catch.

To add to my woes, in the late afternoon one of the finches falls off its perch.

Thursday   24 October
More calls of congratulations from incredulous colleagues and jealous friends. Before international media lands on my doorstep, decide I'd better get my facts straight, so go to the British Museum to bone up on Polish history. I must say, I'm a little

disappointed with my choice of nationality, particularly when I learn that the Poles are the same idiots who tried to rush the Fourth Panzer Division with a herd of horses and a bunch of mops.

Get back to work to find two more finches lying flat on their backs on the bottom of the birdcage, little feet sticking upwards.

Friday   **25 October**
Grapevine continues to spawn tentacles across the European Community. My useless agent calls from the Frankfurt Book Fair terrified her cash cow is going to do a runner to Eastern Europe. Put her mind at ease by saying I'm highly insulted that she'd think I'd mingle with people who eat boiled cabbage and drink cheap-grain alcohol.

My mother puts me in another corner when she rings to ask if 'His Royal Highness' (her words, not mine) would like to spend Christmas in Barnsley with my family. Think cleverly on my feet and tell her he can't as he's got to get back to his homeland to deliver food hampers to the poor and the needy – all 38 million of them.

Another finch falls over head first. Four down, two to go.

Saturday   **26 October**
Forced to lie low at home as I'm supposed to be out having a major public petting session with my fictitious nobleman.

Sunday   **27 October**
Spend painstaking day preparing myself for work tomorrow as it's important I look like I've been seriously ravished all weekend by my Polish paramour. Was going to go riding to get the requisite authentic gait but, given that the horsewhips make me sad and lonely – and prone to thinking of love long lost – give myself a love-bite instead using a vacuum cleaner hose (an old trick I learnt at school). Unfortunately, my Hoover is a deluxe model and has particularly strong suction, so I end up with a welt the size of an ill-informed Third-World nation found to the right of Germany.

Monday   **28 October**

After deliberately not acknowledging my dark glasses, high-necked sweater and carefully contrived sexual dishevelment, Sebastian casually mentions that Tarquin has told him that my author shots are ready to be picked up. Since I know for a fact that Tarquin is single (because I asked him), decide I'd better kill off my phantom Pole as he's cramping my style. Put an end to rumours once and for all by spreading the word via the Gatekeeper that I dropped my titled troglodyte because he expected me to be good in bed and cook, clean and sew.

Last two finches do a double act today and utter their final dying tweets in unison.

Tuesday   **29 October**

Treat Tarquin with my presence at lunch at Zilli's, partly to thank him for doing my photos for nothing, mainly to chat him up and mostly to find out if I'm still revered by my advertising peers. Scan the room and am instantly gratified by frantic waves from most of the functioning alcoholics seated there. At the next table, a famous boxer sits slurping a fruit juice and, whilst being ear-bashed by his manager, keeps shooting me covert glances and flexing his muscles to impress me. Kick Tarquin in the shins before he starts to do something stupid like try to defend my honour. Ever the diplomat, Tarquin winces, rubs his ankle and assures me he wasn't going to do anything of the sort.

Tarquin has brought my author shots along, but is too shy and modest to let me look at them in his presence. Instead, he coyly suggests I wait until I get home to open the envelope.

Wednesday   **30 October**

Spend entire day in bed wallowing in self-pity after seeing the débâcle that was supposed to be my modelling debut. No doubt at Sebastian's request, Tarquin has deliberately made me look like some mentally deranged woman with a very disturbing squint.

In evening, still traumatised by my recent foray into bad lighting and quack photography, decide to stand outside the

Moon Under Water on Leicester Square and count how many
members of the opposite sex can still find it within themselves to
look at me with a telling glint in their eye (32 in 23 minutes).

Return home again with familiar spring back in my step.

Thursday   **31 October**

Whilst busily contemplating how on earth I'm going to write a
book and write my *London Goss* column and hold down a full-
time job in advertising, Eliza drops by my office to say she heard
from a friend of a friend of Sebastian's that Sebastian has been
telling everybody that he heard from a friend of a friend of
Tarquin's that I'm not very photogenic and that Tarquin has
entered one of my pictures into an international gurning
competition. I, of course, refuse to dignify this with a response as
it's typical of the petty rumour-mongering this industry thrives on
and one of the reasons I wish I was no longer a part of it.

Instead, spend the best part of my working day phoning every
advertising blabbermouth I know, saying I am worried about
Sebastian's career as an art director and visual giant, given I know
for a fact he's just been diagnosed with a colour blindness so severe
he has the optical capacity of a dog and, indeed, can only see in
black and white.

PART II

Friday   **1 November**

Today I officially become a self-employed person.

Colleagues stand at the steps of the advertising agency and wave goodbye whilst no doubt trying to hold back their tears. The love-lorn chef from the café next door chases after me, brandishing a day-old Eccles cake in a last-ditch effort to convince me that spotty-faced 20-year-olds are a good catch. Even Thor, that Scandinavian one-time obsession of mine from the computer data processing company on the fourth floor, peers curiously from the balcony above.

I, of course, ignore the lot of them and walk away with as much dignity as one can when being escorted out of the building by two burly security guards and a Doberman. (Will explain my side of the story later. Right now I'm far too distraught, what with having just lost a very lucrative salary and a corner office window. Suffice to say, I will never work in advertising again – not because I *can't* – but because it's full of backstabbing, money-grubbing people who probably all wish to remain anonymous, particularly Sebastian the Judas and Truly Useless Junior Art Director who currently lives at 3 Gilligan Street, Hackney, second window from the right.)

Saturday   **2 November**

Still too distraught to comment.

Sunday   **3 November**

Ditto.

Monday   **4 November**

Foolishly forgetting that I no longer have a ten-to-five job, wake up at five-to-ten to go to work. Then spot the Absolut bottle, aspirin packet, petrol can, cough mixture, model-aeroplane fixative, spoon, foil, syringe, razor blade, mirror and crumpled five-pound note by my bedside table and dimly remember the recent turn of events. Manage to console myself with the thought that I wouldn't be able to do any work anyway as I'm far too hung over.

Brought out of my indolent, unemployed stupor by a phone call in the early afternoon from that treacherous toad, Sebastian. He says he wants to offer his condolences as he was away on a shoot at the Isle of Wight when I was ruthlessly ejected from my ergonomic office chair and had my security pass confiscated. He also says he can't believe our boss reacted so badly when he accidentally let slip that I poisoned the rare Australian chaffinches in the foyer with my tofu burger. I replied that he'd better believe our boss will react badly when he receives the anonymous note I'm about to write regarding Sebastian's flagrant abuse of charge-per-minute sex-line numbers at his employer's expense.

Then ring my solicitor to see if I can wrangle a massive lump-sum compensation pay out from my former place of employ on the grounds of unfair dismissal. My solicitor's got a French accent to die for. Could quite happily listen to him rattle off legal loopholes for hours upon end, except he charges by the minute so I make it brief.

After listening to my proposed sexual harassment case against Sebastian the Snake, my reluctant litigator informs me my claim is a bit tenuous to say the least, since Sebastian shafted me in a metaphorical rather than a literal sense.

In late afternoon, ring solicitor again – this time just to hear his voice.

Tuesday   **5 November**

Trot round to ex-colleague Eliza's place in Camden to find out if my former place of employ is not the same without me. Over a vile vegetarian lunch she's obviously whipped up just to depress me further, Eliza assures me everyone at the ad agency is devastated, the office resembles a mausoleum and Sebastian has had three of his ads rejected by clients.

Get back home feeling slightly better, only to have Teddington drop by, unannounced and uninvited. Having rung my former place of employ on Monday and been informed by the Gatekeeper that I no longer work there, Teddington presumptuously thought I'd been made redundant.

I wasn't made redundant, I snap. I was *sacked*. Redundant

people get elephantine-sized severance cheques, glowing references and guilty looks from employers and colleagues alike. I, on the other hand, got nothing but a particularly murderous glare from my boss and a bill from the toxicology lab. Furthermore, my two week's termination pay was docked because my annual leave was in debit by 14 days.

Job's comforter says he can get me some part-time work behind the bar at the Coach & Horses. But, as I gently point out to him before booting him out my front door, I'm not *that* desperate for money.

Wednesday   **6 November**
Receive an express-couriered £300 invoice from my solicitor's office for my seven-and-half-minute phone session on Monday. In a supremely ironic turn of phrase, the fine print at the bottom of the bill warns if I don't pay up within the seven days specified I may be faced with 'legal action from my solicitor'.

Ring Hortense, my old faithful headhunter, and demand that she get me another well-paying job in advertising. Perhaps still bitter about the severe tongue-lashing I gave her for wasting my valuable time and sick-leave accruals in Singapore recently, she very coolly says that until an advertising agency opens its doors on Mars, she won't be able to help.

In poverty-stricken panic, call my *London Goss* editor and tell him I want double the money for my column. But he pleads poverty too and says he's quite happy for me to stop writing it as his sub-editors are a little peed off with my attitude of late – though all I did was tell them to use the spell-check function on their computers occassionally [*sic*] since they obviously don't know how to use a dictionary.

As a matter of personal dignity and pride, resign on the spot and give him four weeks' notice, as stipulated in the contract he originally made me sign.

Then do dinner with Ferguson at the wrong end of Fulham Road because I can no longer afford to eat on Wanker's Mile. With summer just around the corner, and his latest reticent lover hiding in another, Ferguson has succumbed to the suction pump. Of course, he makes out like he's hobbling around because of a particular ferocious waxing. But he doesn't fool me. I can spot compression bandages under leather trousers a mile off.

Upon hearing about my penurious plight, Ferguson says he can get me reception work at the escort agency as my old pal Phoebe has been promoted. I abruptly cut him off, saying if I want to fend off disgusting old lechers for a living, I can always get another job in advertising.

Thursday   **7 November**
Since my total income will be a big fat nothing in a month's time, I now have no choice but to live off taxpayers indefinitely whilst I devote my precious time to more worthwhile causes like writing my tell-all tome about Mr Dud. After a little preliminary investigation however, am horrified to learn that if I want my handout from the government, I'm going to have to grovel to civil servants. I must have been a complete cow in a former life to attract this kind of karma.

To avoid unnecessary fussing from interfering do-gooders at the DSS, decide I'd better get a doctor's note so I can claim sickness benefits and thus save myself from having to pretend I'm genuinely interested in seeking an honest day's work.

Arrive at Doctor Love's surgery bearing an uncanny resemblance to a nervous wreck (not hard to do after five espressos, half a packet of Marlboros and a quick glance at my Visa statement, *all* before ten in the morning). Wail to my understanding physician about how losing a job is a lot like gaining a boyfriend in that I can neither eat, sleep nor orgasm properly. In a thrice, he declares me 'unfit for work of any kind' and prescribes a year's worth of sedatives which he caringly advises I not take all at once.

Friday   **8 November**
After a particularly deep and heavy night's sleep, get up late, grab clothes brush and insect spray, and prepare to do battle with

assorted scruffs at the Department of Social Security. Give a false name at desk in case anyone waiting in the queue recognises my name when it's screamed out at the top of a sadistic DSS worker's lungs. Of course, I instantly forget my alias, so have to endure hearing the dreadful words 'Janine Jenkins' being bellowed several times before realising it's me who's actually being summoned.

After perusing my non-job application form and making no effort to keep her voice down, the ill-dressed government worker before me sneeringly says that whilst being a drug-dependant flake qualifies me for sickness benefits, sponsoring a wayward child in Africa does not make me eligible for single mother's benefits.

It's not surprising therefore that, after doing quite a lot of yelling back, I stamp out of the building and, in a desperate attempt to make some easy money, take my fully and comprehensively insured Honda Civic hatchback for a reckless pelt towards Marble Arch and other well-known London black spots. Today, however, it seems the Mercedes matrons and Bentley bullies are all on their best behaviour, so I have no option but to career round a giant roundabout at Ludgate Circus in the hope of getting side-swiped by a hurtling truck.

After about two thousand revolutions, only manage to accidentally clip a cyclist whose handlebars and helmet scratched my paintwork but not enough to cover my premium. Start feeling dizzy so drive home again.

Proceed to collect all my gold jewellery (three lockets, four ID bracelets, seven engagement rings, two tiaras, five fillings and one limited edition, meticulously crafted reproduction of a medieval wine goblet), melt the lot down on my gas hob and then try to flog my roughly fashioned ingot to a second-hand jewellers in Hatton Gardens.

My fury is white-hot when a rather patronising evaluator asks me if I've been studying alchemy. It appears that previous loves, dentists and mail-order companies alike have lied to me about the carat value of their pathetic offerings and I have been trying to turn base metals into gold.

Too poor to go out in the evening, so do what all victims of the welfare state do. Stay home and drink myself into oblivion.

Saturday   9 November

Not much to report today since weekends no longer have the same appeal now that I have seven days off per week. Indeed the Saturday and Sunday sports programmes are an unwelcome intrusion upon the weekday soaps and talk shows that I have rapidly become addicted to. (Cannot understand how anyone can spend their entire life kicking a football and still feel like a worthwhile human being with a really interesting job.)

Just as a tautly backsided striker is about to shoot for goal, my gardening pal, Sophie, rudely interrupts. In husky, caring tones, she says she's calling to offer her commiserations about my recent sacking at *London Goss*. 'I wasn't sacked,' I snap. 'I *resigned*.'

Having obviously been fed a crock of misinformation via the *London Goss* publicity machine, Sophie is taken aback by this little bombshell. Indeed, it seems my overly zealous and uncommonly loyal pal has gone way above and beyond the call of duty and quit her gardening column in protest at our mutual editor's riding roughshod over me. This means that I now feel obliged to make a few hurried appreciative grunts in order to get her off the phone before the international deep-sea marlin fishing live broadcast starts. To be perfectly honest, I can't say I'm hugely overwhelmed by her gallant gesture since my soon-to-be ex-*London Goss* editor is hardly going to mourn the loss of Sophie's ramblings on petunias and pergolas.

Thanks to her well-intentioned phone call, though, am once again cruelly reminded that I am rapidly plummeting below the poverty line and had better start tightening purse strings. As soon as the fishing show's finished, scour grocery specials in the newspaper and cab it down to a supermarket in Peckham in order to capitalise on lower demographic discounts.

Aware that gliding down the aisles in my freshly pressed clothes might intimidate the locals, affect a convincing down-trodden shuffle and even chuck a few supermarket own brands in my trolley to make other shoppers feel more at ease.

Sunday   **10 November**
Take to bed with food poisoning after eating no-name can of baked beans.

Monday   **11 November**
Having already stopped eating in order to curtail the cost of living, decide I'd better start spending less on other frivolous items too.

So, with moist eye and heavy heart, write to Sabelo, my African sponsor child, and tell him I'm going to have to cut off his monthly allowance. Am comforted by the thought that at least he's got a roof over his head at the moment as he's back in prison again – this time for getting drunk and disorderly on the bourbon I recently sent him for his ninth birthday.

In afternoon, whilst shopping for half-price postage stamps at local newsagent, am pleased to see headline in *London Goss*'s tabloid rival scream: CIRCULATION SLUMP AT RIVAL TABLOID!!!

Tuesday   **12 November**
After discovering that my dole cheques will not be enough to keep me in cigarettes for four days, let alone a fortnight, endeavour to roll my own. Consequently waste half a day wrestling with a packet of Rizlas and soon realise why the unemployed don't have time to look for jobs.

Slam my tobacco pouch down in fit of frustration and decide to go sponge some manufactured ciggies at Piccadilly Circus. During the begging débâcle that ensues, soon come to the conclusion that people with jobs are cruel, unfeeling misers who get particularly narky about doling out smokes and cab fares to 'long-haired layabouts'.

Just when I've finally completed my long walk back home and put my weary feet up in anticipation of a marathon of afternoon soaps, I receive one of those spine-tinglingly awful 'blast from the past' phone calls. It's from Angel, an old school friend of mine.

I have been deliberately – and successfully – avoiding her for the past 12 years as she serves as a stark and bleak reminder of the fact I used to go to a comprehensive school. In *Barnsley*. Apparently,

Angel now lives in London too. But, unlike me, she hasn't managed to escape her less-than-illustrious past. She tells me she's presently flatting in Tottenham, dating a plumber, and working part-time as a jewellery party-plan consultant.

In her horribly familiar Yorkshire burr, Angel asks if I'd like to catch up for some 'grub'. I'm about to abruptly decline in more refined southern tones, but then she adds it's her shout. Instantly acquiesce and agree to meet her this Sunday at Spaghetti Junction in Enfield, because I don't want to be seen with her at anywhere in Soho.

Wednesday   **13 November**

During a particularly absorbing re-run of *Prisoner: Cell Block H*, my useless agent rings to nag me about the manuscript she is supposed to be delivering to my publisher and I am supposed to have written. Cunningly skirt around the issue by hanging up on her.

Anyway, I'm too weak to do anything remotely literary-like during daylight hours as I've now gone without food for nigh on three days. Indeed, am only roused from the depths of my couch-potato state in the evening by the promise of a free meal at Quaglino's, compliments of Teddington who's a starving author too, except, unlike me, he actually needs to lose some weight. And he's never been published.

While his ever-present muse looks on dourly, Teddington tries to get into my good books by saying I don't have to order from the fixed-price menu. He then has the temerity to start grilling me about my invaluable publishing contacts under the pretext that he's interested in my exciting new literary career. Manage to fob him off by choking on a lobster claw which I accidentally down in my all-out feeding frenzy.

After applying a quick and efficient Heimlich manoeuvre (and vexing me no end because he beat an infinitely more attractive nearby waiter to it), Teddington informs me he's thinking of applying for a grant since he's finding it hard to write whilst working full-time. Taking this as the deliberate dig that it is about my own non-working status, wait until Teddington's seen the restaurant bill's grand total and, when he starts hyperventilating, return his previous first-aid favour and engage him in an extremely firm stranglehold. Then casually ask for more details about the grant.

Thursday   14 November
Apply for Teddington's grant in valiant effort to save British taxpayers from wasting good money on bad bets like him.

Since I suspect funds will be unfairly awarded to applicants with greater literary pretensions than my own, have accidentally memorised an entire chapter of *War and Peace* which I perchance found on my bookshelf, so it can't be helped if some words, phrases and, indeed, whole paragraphs unconsciously creep into my own submission. However, do take extreme care to change all the main characters' names in order to avoid charges of plagiarism from uptight members of the literati.

Friday   15 November
Still debating as to whether 'Dick', 'Jane' and 'Spot' pack quite the same punch as 'Pierre', 'Natasha' and 'Napoleon'.

Saturday   16 November
In a bid to subsidise my new career as a penniless writer who has not as yet received a whopping great Arts Council grant, try my hand at busking down Sloane Square tube.

Half-way through a haunting rendition of *Greensleeves* in C# minor, spot sure-fire meal ticket gawping at me in that idiotic way men do when they see a girl blowing hard down a descant recorder whilst clad in flimsy attire. Distressingly enough, I never get to thank him for the £20 note he reverently places in the Prada bag at my feet because I'm too busy struggling violently with a pair of plain – and fully clothed – policewomen clearly peeved by my popularity with the opposite sex.

Luckily, when they try to bring me in for questioning (and trumped-up charges for lewd misconduct and indecent exposure) at my local police station, my old sergeant at the desk recognises me straight away and, perhaps still unable to come to terms with the painful reminder of what he's been missing all this time, throws me out into the street again.

Spend latter part of the evening crying into cheap paper towels in the girl's loo at Zilli's because during the former part I discovered I am *persona non grata* in the main bar. Foolishly thinking that my ex-advertising colleagues previously bought me drinks on account of my vibrant personality and amazing good looks, I've come to the rude realisation they were only after me for my like-minded ability to prattle on ad infinitum about my huge salary and genius award-winning ads.

Sunday   17 November

Having had to spend all my busking money on buying my own house whites last night, am forced to stoop to Harvey Nicks' counter and surrender myself to the mercies of a Lancôme lackey in order to bum a free make-over so I can face an evening with Angel.

Thankfully, I'm only meeting her at the Spaghetti Junction in Enfield, so I don't have to dress to impress. Indeed, I sashay in wearing an amusing little number I cleverly whipped up using a bin-bag, some clingfilm and a couple of dishcloths. (It was either that or stealing a twinset from Oxfam and I'm not big on stale-smelling hand-me-downs trying to pass themselves off as retro chic.)

I must say, the skeleton in my closet is looking distinctly heiferesque these days. Even against the backdrop of a dozen suburban housewives, the once ferret-framed Angel still manages to resemble a small whale. I'm not particularly overwhelmed by her rustic lover either. Bogie Boy might be a six-foot stud five years her junior who keeps giving me appreciative once-overs all night, but that doesn't make up for the fact I saw him put tomato sauce on his fettucine carbonara.

Monday   18 November

Wake up late afternoon because I didn't get to bed until four this morning, so busy was I watching telly and wondering who in the world would be stupid enough to sign up for all those courses screened on the Open University.

Tuesday   **19 November**

Tutorial notes for architecture, modern history and maths arrive express delivery today. Since I can't afford to pay for them myself, ring my brother Biggles in Senegal. He makes me promise I'll use his cash to pay bills rather than squander it on passing whims as I am wont to do when he gives me £1,000. Loudly protest that I'm a changed woman, whilst quietly thanking God for making all men such gullible idiots.

Wednesday   **20 November**

Without wishing to gloat, it seems my nemesis, Sebastian, has come drastically undone. According to agency mole, Eliza, unable to successfully mimic my strong leadership skills and brilliant creative mind, Seb Savant is completely incapable of sound judgement and coherent ads. It has also come to pass that his so-called 'uncle' and very important client at my former place of employ has just found out that Sebastian is not his blood nephew after all. To cut short a very long, highly confidential, dreadfully embarrassing and incredibly interesting story about love, lust, adulterous mothers and extensive DNA tests, Sebastian the Bastard has just been sacked.

Wait a decorous five minutes upon hearing this, then call Lucifer's love-child to find out how badly he's doing. (Have to ring him at home since I cannot call him at work because he no longer has a job.) His disgraced mother answers the phone and says Sebastian is indisposed as he has an unsightly, stress-induced skin ailment – no doubt induced by the sheer terror of looking for another job without the aid of a kindly uncle in the business. Get off the phone, mood even more dramatically uplifted.

Thursday   **21 November**

Whilst watching a personnel recruitment expert on a breakfast show declare that career women are far too reticent about asking their employers for the money they deserve, my *London Goss* editor rings to grovel and beg me to continue writing my column, presumably because advertisers have been leaving in their droves now that word has got around that I will soon be bidding adieu to my readers.

Make him sweat more than he usually does by saying I'll think about it – though only if I can have quadruple the money. Since my very reasonable demand comes in at slightly less than the promotional budget *London Goss* had earmarked for a national subscription drive in a last-ditch attempt to boost circulation figures, my editor agrees at once. Indeed, I swear I can almost hear the tinkle of dandruff as he nods fervently down the phone. Later, I have to miss a gripping episode of *Neighbours* because I've promised to meet up with Sophie at Harvey Nick's Fifth Floor Bar (which I can afford to frequent again now I am at last a well-remunerated columnist).

Unaware of my financial victory this morning, Sophie confides she recently told my *London Goss* editor that no matter how much he pleads with her, she will not resume writing her horticultural column unless I am allowed to continue writing mine. Wisely refrain from replying that my editor will probably be unable to afford to re-hire her now he's paying me a five-figure net sum per week. In the evening, have to tear myself away from the telly, because Teddington and his muse are trying to curry favour again by taking me to a new Russian restaurant where Ivan the terrifying waiter still thinks he's in the Gulags. In a thoroughly undemocratic manner, he orders me what to eat, issues me wine not of my own choosing and glares fiercely when I refuse to eat the unasked-for side-order of blinis. By the end of my pre-ordained and decidedly proletarian meal, I'm a gibbering wreck and have to take at least 20 of Doctor Love's sedatives with my double espresso.

After much prompting from his muse, Teddington makes the most of my chemically altered, mild-mannered state and nervously asks if I would pass on his latest piece of unpublishable tripe to my agent. Even at my most benign, I can still feel the bile rise at this latest imposition upon my good name. Fortunately, my anger combined with five stiff vodkas and half a bottle of Valium prove a potent mix and I conveniently pass out at the table before giving him my answer or settling my bill.

Friday   22 November

After a thoroughly traumatic overnight stay at the local psychiatric hospital, and having assured the sceptical staff there that my near-death experience was purely accidental since I've always intended on going out with a bang, not with a series of drug-induced whimpers, am finally released from the constraints of a rather badly designed bed-jacket and allowed back into the real world at eight o'clock this morning.

Get home, check letter box and find a postcard from Calliope who I haven't heard from in quite some time, even though it's her turn to call. In extraordinarily cryptic tones, she says she is having a *wonderful time in Algeria* with her *new Fundamentalist boyfriend* and that she *really wishes I was here.* Even in my currently befuddled state, this news worries me somewhat. I had made Calliope promise she wouldn't get a steady boyfriend without consulting me first (a commitment I try to extract from all my friends so that I have time to nip potentially long-term relationships in the bud and thus be guaranteed a choice of drinking partners on a Saturday night).

By evening am feeling clear-headed again, so head off to the University Arms in Bloomsbury, intent upon scabbing drinks from the younger, more naive male patrons, thus perhaps finding my own steady boyfriend. Latch on to an amateur ornithologist who counts white-fronted geese for the Thames Water Authority and feel obliged to take him home after he pays for all my tequilas. Romantic progress is hindered somewhat when he spies an extremely rare breed of owl nesting in the tree outside my living-room window. Indeed, Bird-brain spends the midnight hour clucking and hooting at his feathered friend whilst I lounge seductively, albeit a little petulantly.

Saturday   23 November

Open my curtains only to be blinded by the glare of a dozen

fluorescent anoraks huddled in the park below and peering my way through binoculars. At first, am secretly flattered that word about my massive desirability has spread so quickly since last night – despite the fact I threw my date out into the night without an informal kiss goodnight. But, when I realise they're actually observing the stupid owl, race down to the park with neither hair nor make-up in place, flapping my arms about and shrieking demonically, and soon have them all scarpering back to their bicycles.

Mission accomplished, go back indoors again, and spend eight hours getting dressed to the nines because I'm meeting with my agent for refreshments in Soho tonight and I like making her feel inferior. Suspect she's starting to panic on my behalf about my now overdue book deadline and is hoping her spectre-like presence will scare me into writing faster.

Unfortunately, having got wind of this on Thursday, no doubt by prying it out of me when I was semi-conscious in the ambulance, Teddington knocks on my door in the afternoon eagerly clutching his manuscript (*How To Get Published Against All Odds*) and asks if I can hand it to my agent. After fervently assuring him I'll do my best and slamming the door in his face, toss the manuscript to one side, then head off to Browns determined to drink at least 15 per cent's worth of agent's commission.

Sunday   24 November

Hideous hangover notwithstanding, today I try to make a start on my tell-all tome because last night my idiot agent told me she's arranged an editorial conference call between me and my Scottish-based publisher next week.

To be perfectly honest, I'm finding it extremely difficult to turn a three-and-a-half minute non-event into a rollercoaster epic. However by mid-morning, I've completed my tome's title – *3½ Minutes (Can Seem Like A Lifetime)* – so decide to reward myself by taking a break to watch one of my favourite talk shows.

Today's topic is all about how modest people are more likeable than others. So, in the afternoon, whilst promenading round Hyde Park with ex-colleague, Eliza, pretend not to notice all the admiring stares from fathers pushing buggies. Meantime, Eliza regales me with more salacious gossip from my former place of employ: apparently when my mortal enemy Sebastian was given the boot, he had to be coaxed out of the building by an emergency counsellor *and* a registered nurse.

Arrive home in a (for once) totally natural state of euphoria, only to spy more bird nerds below my window.

Monday   **25 November**
After receiving complaints from my neighbours, all of whom think the lunatics crawling through the grass with high-powered lenses and bird seed are some of my more avid admirers, ring my local council and demand that the tree outside my window be felled immediately. An insolent desk clerk tells me this isn't possible as conservation officials are now considering turning the park and my block of flats into a bird sanctuary and multi-storey theme restaurant respectively.

Appalled to hear this since I refuse to be ousted from my garret in favour of a swarm of beady-eyed beaks, take the axe that I keep under my bed to deter unwanted amorous advances and proceed to chop the tree down myself. Many back-breaking hours later, get rid of the incriminating evidence by heaving the wood up to my garret and burning it in my grate – using Teddington's unsolicited manuscript as kindling.

Tuesday   **26 November**
Wake up with stinging eyes and a horrendous cough because, unbeknownst to me, my chimney flue was sealed off.

At the surgery later, dishy Doctor Love seems quite smitten by my feebly feminine state, despite the fact I am covered from head to toe in soot. He pretends he's checking my lungs, though I could swear he was leering at their more buoyant outer parts. To impress him further, ask for a bulk-pack of birth control repeat prescriptions. Then take them and my sedatives home.

Wake up late afternoon feeling rather sluggish but nonetheless attempt to pen *3½ Minutes*. Half an hour later, extensive literary research via telly, phone and kettle, comes to a grinding halt when all my power is cut off.

Wednesday   27 November
Spend the day as a homeless person wandering aimlessly up and down King's Road whilst waiting for my electricity, phone and gas to be put back on (the heartless beasts at London Electricity, British Telecom and the Gas Board refused to believe my story about how the cheques were in the post but must have got lost by the halfwits at Royal Mail).

Seek refuge for a while in Dillons's humour section, flicking through *Women are from Venus, Men are from Mars* and trying to work out who actually reads such chauvinistic drivel. Manager soon asks me to leave because my snorts and chortles are disturbing the squatters in the nearby Spirituality & Inner Peace section.

Proceed to pursue more cheap entertainment by torturing a sales assistant at Russell & Bromley's. Try on 26 pairs of mules before tossing them all carelessly aside and walking out of shop empty-handed.

Afterwards, move on to Coffee Republic where I inadvertently annoy waiters by lingering over a single glass of complimentary tap water (with free slice of lemon) during their busy lunch hour. By late afternoon, I'm thirsty again. Head for home to the well-heeled Blakes Hotel and lie in wait of some eternally hopeful middle-aged businessman who may want to buy me a couple of drinks with no strings attached.

Thursday   28 November
Leave Blakes bright and early after stealing complimentary soap from bathroom.

Friday   29 November
Just when I think things can't get any worse, I suddenly find myself

writing a newsletter for the party plan company where Angel works. The marketing manager who usually carries out such lowly tasks has come down with a severe allergy from wearing Jools & Co's cheap-plated baubles. When Angel called me this morning to enlist my superior literary talents, I tell her I'm only doing it because I've just frittered away most of my unemployment benefits upon extortionate reconnection fees and exorbitant business expenses.*

Of course, now that I am back in the world of advertising, albeit as a lowly freelancer, I can walk into the Zilli's with my head held relatively high and bereft of a paper bag.

*See Monday, 18 November.

Saturday   **30 November**
According to a reliable advertising industry source I brushed lips with last night, Sebastian has a deadly flesh-eating disease and is therefore not long for this world. This means I am forced to do the right thing, pick up a bunch of poor people's flowers from 7-Eleven and drive all the way to Sebastian and his mother's place in Hackney to pay my last respects.

To my utter disgust, I find Old Scales is perfectly alive and well and merely has a bad case of hives, which unfortunately has not stopped him attempting to put his pathetic excuse of an art portfolio together. Upon spying me at the doorway to the dark and dank squalor that is his bedroom, Sebastian piteously mewls on about my flagrant abuse of my role as a social commentator and asks that I refrain from writing 'horrible, untrue things' in my *London Goss* column as he has become the 'laughing stock' amongst his peers.

I storm out in high dudgeon, enraged at such unfair accusations since, like most self-respecting journalists on national morning tabloids, I do have what is commonly known as 'ethics'.

Sunday   **1 December**
For lack of anything better to do than write my book, head off to Soho determined to drain the Coach & Horses dry, courtesy of

junior barman, Teddington. Opportunistic as always, Teddington makes the most of my well-connected appearance at the bar by asking me in unnecessarily eager tones if I've shown his manuscript to my agent, like I'd promised.

Not wishing to break it to him that I used his papery pile of drivel to cut the cost of my winter fuel bills, I lie and say that I did indeed hand it to her and she in turn suggested that Teddington look into vanity publishing. No sooner has my distraught friend fled back to where he belongs to rinse out my empty glasses, I notice his muse shooting me a poisonous look from across the room. She's obviously had to start waiting on tables in an effort to boost the joint household income. Shoot her a poisonous look back because I really don't think she should be encouraging Teddington's woeful career by helping him out financially.

Monday   **2 December**
Have just had an extremely threatening call from my thus-far patient and understanding publisher. Not content with the title page and back-cover blurb I handed across the table, she's now got the gall to demand the bits in between.

Well aware that as an *artiste* I am expected to come up with a highly creative excuse as to why I haven't finished *3½ Minutes*, I told her I've been suffering from a particularly vicious bout of post-traumatic stress disorder following my sexual ordeal with Mr Dud. After a painfully long and ominously drawn-out silence, my publisher said that if I don't deliver at least half of the manuscript to her by next Wednesday, I will be 'forced' to give back my advance.

Easier said than done, I felt wont to retort, given that most of it is securely locked away in cash registers and bar tills up and down King's Road.

Tuesday   **3 December**
During early morning search for literary inspiration and an empty council bin within which to dispose of three empty Absolut bottles, spot rogue Porsche in my block of flat's carpark. Further

investigations reveal a tell-tale removal van parked outside the main entrance foyer, closely followed by a gorgeous new male tenant whom I then tail upstairs to the constantly vacated apartment directly opposite my mine.

Afterwards I'm way too distracted to work so while away rest of day plotting all kinds of sordid but sensual scenarios.

Wednesday   **4 December**

Spend many unproductive hours trying to write *3½ Minutes* whilst crouched down in the corridor outside my garret in the hope of catching the attention of my eminently fanciable neighbour. Creative process is impeded somewhat by pesky pals and their petty problems. Each time the phone rings, have to dash back indoors and risk breaking my neck over the extension cord that trails from my living-room wall socket to my laptop in the corridor.

First it's Angel howling like a baby because she's just found out she's about to have one in two months time (having left school halfway through the sex-education syllabus she thought her extraordinary weight-gain was due to pre-menstrual bloating rather than pre-natal blubber). Then it's Sophie's less-than-dulcet tones growling on the line to say she's enormously glad to hear I've got my column contract renewed and so is back on board with *London Goss,* though on radically less money than previous. And, finally, it's Teddington to blubber on about something, though I didn't quite catch what because I hung up on him after tersely telling him to go tell it to the Samaritans because I'm extremely busy at the minute trying to meet *a book deadline.*

Thursday   **5 December**

Venture out to local library determined to mine its shelves for ideas in order to flesh out my salacious tome. Well-meaning librarian misunderstands my missive completely and points me to Hemingway, Chaucer and a bunch of books by South Americans with long-winded names.

After finding my own way to the Love & Relationships section, end up at counter armed with *The Rules*. Spend a few hours at home immersed in this, the definitive guide on how to capture a man's heart in the nineties, and resolve to keep a few tips in mind whilst I continue my coquettish vigil in the corridor.

Finally, at about eight in the evening, my virile neighbour steps out of the lift, briefcase in hand. He looks at me with a sardonically raised eyebrow, beats a manly retreat into his abode and then shuts his door in a captivating way. Feel like demanding to know where he's been and why he's home so late but don't wish to pressure him so early on in the relationship. Instead, play by *The Rules* and try to make him jealous by going out for the evening with another man. Never mind that I'm having dinner at the Star of India with suspiciously fresh-faced Ferguson and mutton-dressed-as-Marvin.

Ferguson is madly in love with Marvin, whom he met last night on Clapham Common. Sadly, even though Ferguson has loaned him his best pair of leather trousers, I don't think the relationship will last, given that Marvin is 50, married with five kids and has a very high-profile job in the diplomatic corps. Plus he's a Canadian – albeit one with a sense of humour. Indeed, he laughs politely at all my jokes about Canadians without one.

Typically, Ferguson tries to steal my spotlight by hastily interrupting and asking me if I've seen Phoebe recently. Apparently, I should be prepared for a shock, he titters, as my old friend has changed dramatically. Much to the mirth of Marvin (and the dismay of Ferguson), I drolly reply I hope that Ferguson's fetish for refusing to age gracefully hasn't rubbed off on her.

Friday   6 December
Dutiful Eliza comes round during her lunchbreak from the ad agency, armed with a cordless drill. Since she hasn't had a man around her house in over three years, she's learnt to become extremely efficient at carrying out unfeminine chores. Needless to say, I'm making the most of her enduring misfortune by insisting she bore a small hole through my front door so I can court my new crush from a more discreet vantage point.

Eliza timorously suggests I'm mad and that I should just bang on his door and demand a date. I retort that there is nothing so repellent as a woman who actively chases a man. Eliza just looks at me dumbfounded. Hand her my well-thumbed copy of *The Rules* because she clearly doesn't have a clue when it comes to romantic etiquette.

Late in the afternoon, take a mail-break in order to give my tired eyes a rest from peephole duties. Consequently discover a letter in my letter box from the Arts Council. It seems my recent application for a grant has been rejected because my work wasn't up to standard. This news cheers me up immensely. It just goes to prove my theory that Tolstoy is extremely overrated.

Saturday   **7 December**
Because it is fitting for a lady to be intentionally unavailable to the man she intends to marry, I have very reluctantly agreed to vacate my garret for the weekend and stay overnight at Sophie's family farm as she's got a friend's party to attend nearby. End up at some glass-blower's 'studio' in Gloucestershire which, tragically, is many miles from an even remotely appealing member of the male species. Indeed, at first glance the place appears to be populated purely by bow-legged beards doing wheelies on 500cc bikes along the front patio.

At second glance, and with the aid of the four cans of Hooch proffered to me, it still appears that way. The only talent worth ogling is a moody goatherd type who just simmers in the corner whilst all the country women in the barn queue to chat him up. Being a city girl, I, of course, act alluringly aloof by totally ignoring him. He in turn totally ignores me, though I did catch him gazing in overt admiration when I downed a freshly moulded yard-glass full of beer in three and a half seconds flat.

Retire to Sophie's family farm at about two in the morning, slightly the worse for wear. Sophie's eager-to-please mother seems fairly surprised when I head straight for the guest room. She asks me if I wouldn't feel more comfortable sleeping in Sophie's childhood bedroom.

Certainly not, I reply, somewhat shortly. I'll never get a good night's sleep if I'm surrounded by tacky Tonka Toy truck posters and Action Man mobiles.

Sunday   8 December

Spend five hideously hung over hours traipsing through an orchard, a duck pond, a cowshed, and a tractor auction because I am stupidly relying upon Sophie to do the right thing by a dear, severely sick friend and drive me straight back to London.

Sophie seems to be in a particularly grim mood, too. Of course, this may have something to do with the fact that when my well-built pal appeared at my door with an odd look in her eyes in the twilight hours, I thought one of the cows had found its way into the farmhouse, and hurled my bedside jug of water at it.

Once Sophie's seen fit to finally drop me off at home, with nary a smile or even a gruff goodbye, I immediately perch myself in my regular position behind the hole in my front door. Patience pays off at around ten in the evening when I finally spy my handsome prey. Unfortunately, it appears he's a single dad. Indeed, I observe him leaving his apartment with a small boy in tow, the latter carrying an overnight bag. This means I will now have to lay romantic obsessions to rest since I am definitely *not* ready for a family yet.

Monday   9 December

At seven o'clock this morning, I receive an extremely strange call from my mother asking me why I haven't yet collected her and my father from King's Cross station.

One hour later, and between several awkward silences at the lost-luggage counter, am horrified to learn my parents have travelled all the way from Barnsley in second-class seats under the mistaken belief that I'd agreed they could stay with me for the week.

I explain in even tones that I don't actually remember making a rather flip offer of free accommodation and guided tour of London. And, even if I had, I certainly wouldn't have expected them to be insensitive enough to take me up on it, especially when they know how busy I am – what with my overdue book deadline and my increasingly desperate quest for a man with a low sperm count.

My father looks ready to chuck an embarrassingly public apoplectic fit when I guide him and my mother gently but firmly into the ticket purchase queue. Try to calm him down by reminding him of all the lovely scenery he'll see on the way back to Barnsley.

Spend rest of afternoon bedridden with what I think may be delayed guilt about my actions. Fortunately, though, by early evening I've managed to flashback to some of my many childhood traumas (including the one about how I was cruelly abandoned in a shopping centre without my parents' credit card when I was only *18*), and realise I have every right to be a dysfunctional daughter.

Tuesday   **10 December**

Literary endeavours torn asunder once again when my ex-boss from my former place of employ rings to ask for a favour. Thinking he means 'favour' as in 'writing-an-ad-and-charging-his-agency-a-fortune favour', I jump from my home-office laptop at the chance to help him out. Am only going to do it because I enjoy seeing grown men grovel at my feet after they realise the errors of their ways.

No doubt having come to the startling conclusion that it was Sebastian and not I who was the source of all evil and bad ads, my boss will probably take me to our old watering hole, Zilli's, and try to beg me back, having not found anyone as adept at the printed word (hardly surprising since most advertising copywriters can't actually *write*). I am, of course, going to graciously tell him that whilst I am now above penning prices for pilchards, I am willing to let bygones be bygones. Am then going to try to drink him out of business – no small feat considering he's had a 20-year head start on me in this particular sport.

Naturally, my displeasure knows no end when I arrive at the ad agency only to find out that my ex-boss simply wants me to act as an unpaid extra and fill up one of the many vacant desks in order to convince a very important client that, despite the recent staff mass exodus, the place is still a hive of activity. Things must be getting desperate because even the cleaner is parked in front of a Mac, staring in bewilderment at the mouse. (The visiting client appears fairly flummoxed too when, having asked for a demonstration, the cleaner misunderstands and starts polishing the screen.)

Fortunately, all I have to do is hide behind *Marie Claire* magazine and pretend that I'm studying competitor's ads – just like I used to do in the good old days, except, of course, in the good old days, I used to actually get *paid*.

I must say, am not greatly amused to discover that the Gate-keeper has taken over half of mine and Sebastian's old office. Apparently, agency funds are so low she's now trying to do my job as well. Quite frankly I don't fancy her chances, especially not after I order her back to the switchboard.

Even Eliza's job description as accounts clerk has broadened to incorporate production manager, account executive and, worse still, office tea lady. Indeed, I have to send her scuttling off to the staff kitchen to dispense with the revolting rosehip brew she's just tried to serve me.

Wednesday   11 December
Today I have to come up with a plausible excuse as to why I still haven't contributed so much as a single word to *3½ Minutes*. So, after much careful deliberation, I've decided to fake my own abduction.

Place a handkerchief over my telephone mouthpiece, dial up the publishing house in Edinburgh and, in appropriately throaty tones, ask to be put through to my publisher. Grand plan stymied when I am informed she's had to head down south on an urgent business matter and won't be back for at least a week. Hang up hugely aggrieved by what is grossly unprofessional behaviour on her part.

Thursday   12 December
Ring my agent to complain about my unreliable, irresponsible publisher. Temporarily forgetting which side her bread is buttered

on, my agent says it's all my fault. As my manuscript is now a month overdue, my Scottish publisher has had to dash over the border in order to placate a particularly bellicose printer whose machinery overheated after being left idle for so long. Snap at my agent that it's the printer's own stupid fault for using locally produced and poorly manufactured goods and whose side is she on anyway? My agent immediately tries to save her neck and future earnings by inviting me to her Christmas party next week. Act as non-committal as I can because I know she's counting on me being there as I'm her most celebrated client. Detect a note of panic in her voice when I hum and haw about it for some time before graciously declining.

In the afternoon, my pregnant friend, Angel, drops by, flumps down on my until-now sag-free sofa, to announce she's getting married to Bogie Boy. If this isn't bad enough, she then proposes I be the matron of honour since I'm obviously too past it to qualify as a bridesmaid. Cannot wholeheartedly refuse as I'm her 'oldest' friend (or so she likes to think), so grudgingly accept, taking care to lay down some stringent ground rules first: the best man must be single and attractive; I must be allowed to wear a short black frock of my own choosing; and I mustn't be required to show up for any tedious pre-wedding rehearsals.

After Angel's signed the pre-nups that I've hastily scribbled up, demand to know how she managed to locate my place of residence, as I'd deliberately given her the wrong one when I spoke to her last. Angel replies that, after driving around the other side of town for many hours to no avail, she rang up *London Goss* and said she was a fan of mine.

Am outraged at this breach of security on the paper's part. I'd left them under strict instructions to only let strangers of the male variety have my real address.

Friday   13 December

Have not sent anyone a Christmas card yet, so hellbent am I upon separating my real friends from the hangers-on and celebrity-worshippers that crowd my life daily. And, according to my tally thus far, my sneaking suspicions appear to be true – I'm surrounded only by people who like me for what I can offer them, not for what they can give me. Indeed, the double-sided sticky tape I have adhered across the entire length of my living-room wall is bare, save for a couple of pissed-off moths.

Still, I refuse to panic just yet and instead laze away the morning hanging nonchalantly around my letter box.

When a typically tardy and particularly insolent postal-service worker sees fit to arrive late afternoon, we hurl a couple of well-chosen festive insults at each other before he hands me nothing but two bills and an unwelcome reminder note from my mother in the shape of a 'Happy Birthday, Dear Daughter' card. This sends me into a deeply depressive state since I now have to face the fact that, a week come Saturday, I will be 30 years old.

It also means I have a piddling seven days left in which to give up immature, irresponsible habits like smoking, drinking and gratuitous sex.

Saturday   **14 December**
Wake up with a hacking cough and some strange man manacled to my bed posts. How he got there is completely beyond me since the last thing I recall was sitting in some seedy Soho nightclub at three o'clock this morning, drinking to forget my impending dotage.

Am forced to leave him spreadeagled upon my best sheets because I can't find the keys to the cuffs and, besides, I've got to go spend my tax refund. (After an extremely protracted and thoroughly malicious audit, the people at the Inland Revenue saw fit to squeeze a £2,000 cheque into my letter box today. Fortunately, most civil servants live outside London, so fail to realise that Paul Smith and Dolce & Gabbana are neither legal advisers nor financial planners. And it's not my fault if they also work under the mistaken belief that Habitat sell office filing cabinets.)

Blow my entire windfall down King's Road on a new winter wardrobe and matching home furnishings. Then, after taking care to file all the receipts for the next financial year in my newly acquired office in-tray-cum-Japanese handcarved jewellery box, race back home to call a locksmith.

Once unshackled, my ungrateful guest makes good his dash for freedom, leaving me no time to slip him his bus fare home or ask him his name. Locksmith also seems a bit bemused by events, especially when I refuse to pay him and instead request that he invoice the landlord for services rendered to a dodgy front-door lock.

Sunday   15 December
Spend much of the day attempting to scrape candle wax off mattress whilst grumbling out loud about the tediousness of it all. At the same time, secretly congratulate myself for still looking innocent enough and therefore young enough to lure an unsuspecting male into doing things he previously only read about in his girlfriend's *Cosmo*.

Things take a turn for the worse when Teddington makes an unwelcome visit. Dripping tears of monumental self-pity all over my brand-new coffee table from Aero (receipt no. 23, office desk), he sorrowfully informs me his muse has left him, declaring him too easily manipulated by his friends and a pushover with people in general.

Realising that it's sometimes better to be cruel to be kind, especially where Teddington's concerned, I tell him I think it's got more do with the fact he's such an abject failure and she's sick to death of supporting him. Then make him take me out for dinner at the French House in return for having to listen to him snivel for so long.

Monday   16 December
Discover three prematurely grey hairs sprouting from my fringe. Am not overtly thrilled by this as I was hoping to ensnare a boyfriend within the next five days so I can score a decent birthday present.

Immediately head down King's Road to hair salon for the shallow and superficial, only to come across fanciful Ferguson ensconced in foil. He grudgingly admits he's flying off to Morocco today to get over his old lover Marvin and so he's getting his hair highlighted in order that it looks naturally sun-kissed when he gets back to London next week. Following the trainee colourist's mishap with the toner, I'll be interested to see how Ferguson explains the non-UV salmon-pink effect to all his butch friends in Marrakesh.

After my own expert follicle flunkey has plucked the offending silver threads from my naturally flaxen locks, get home, check letter box and am mortified to discover I have received only *two* Christmas cards. They are from my accountant and solicitor respectively, the cost of which will no doubt be billed to me next quarter. At least my golden-larynxed solicitor has thought to send me one of those voice-message cards. Hugely excited at hearing his well-modulated French tones for free, race straight to the phone and dial the number with trembling fingers. My disappointment is crushing when I hear his Brummie secretary yabbering 'Merry Christmus from all of us 'ere at Woodcock, Baum & Dujon'.

Tuesday   **17 December**

Two more unsolicited Christmas cards arrive today; one is from my laundry man, who's clearly angling for a Christmas bonus, and the other's from, *quel surprise*, Sebastian. Judging from the hand-sketched atrocity I hold before me, it seems that 1) he still can't draw properly, 2) he wants to call a truce and 3) he's relying heavily upon me being full of yuletide spirit.

'Please let's make up' implores the speech bubble ballooning from a badly rendered reindeer. Sighing heavily, put the card back in its envelope and write 'Not at this address' on the front and 'Bog off, Rudolph' on the back.

Wednesday   **18 December**

After Royal Mail bypasses my place altogether today, my deep-rooted insecurities finally come to the fore and, in an innate and pathetic desire to be liked indiscriminately, pick up a bulk-pack of Christmas cards from Woolworths to send out to all my so-called 'friends'.

Then, having taken the art of procrastination to its nth degree, spend rest of the day holed up at home attempting to churn out a book faster than Barbara Cartland on speed because I have a feeling my publisher is going to enquire as to the whereabouts of *3½ Minutes* when I arrive in Edinburgh tomorrow – particularly since I'd promised to give it to her only if she forked out for my flight.

By midnight and with the aid of a wealth of previous sexual encounters, fleshed out with an overdose of adverbs, adjectives and prepositions, have managed to bang out an entire 50,000-word manuscript.

I must say, I can't see how it takes other authors so long to write books.

Thursday   19 December

Today, am in Edinburgh which – for the benefit of any tax department moles reading this – is for *business purposes only*. Haven't bothered packing any of my usual clothes as they're all designer labels and, instead, am wearing a sensible Scotch House tweed ensemble because I don't wish to be mistaken for a London tourist and be mugged on the streets. A wise choice too given that I have been checked into a tourist tenement slum that seems abnormally proud of the fact each room comes with its very own kettle. Humour management and drink five cups of instant coffee whilst waiting for my agent (who has decided to tail me up to Scotland to make sure I stick to my word and put in an appearance) to whisk me off to Malmaison for something stronger.

Soon get stuck into the house bubbly which I let my agent shout me, since I'm the one who's really paying for it. She jokes about how she wishes I would write another book so she could develop a Bolly habit. Tempted to tell her that given my current productivity levels, she'll probably end up on meths.

Friday   20 December

In morning, cab it down to Princes Street to buy something smart and sensible for the meet-and-greet-and-hand-over-the-manuscript with my publisher this afternoon. Old habits die hard and I end up wedged into little black designer dress that could double as a shirt if I ever did care to wear it with jacket and trousers.

At the publishing house, staff stampede the boardroom – so eager are they to shake an imminently famous author's hand. My killjoy publisher promptly asks me for the manuscript, snatches it out of my hand, throws it to the production manager who whisks it off to the typesetters.

When the French-onion dip runs out, upper and middle management reluctantly depart and lumber me with minions from the publicity department for the night. We hail a cab and set off for a night of drunken debauchery at the Basement.

On our typically tumultuous journey in a suicidal Scottish cab, spot an especially attractive young man fool enough to brave the pedestrian crossing in rush-hour traffic. Taking fate into my own hands, grab the wheel and turn it sharply towards my intended. Once I've got his attention, slam on the brakes to avert disaster and to ensure my target hurls himself on to and into the cab windscreen, landing smack-bang in the middle of my lap.

Fortunately, I am not hurt, though I must admit I was somewhat shaken. Invite my recently introduced guest to the Basement, but he begs off with a headache. Reluctantly drop him off at the nearest hospital only after he's handed over his share of the fare. Then give cab driver bogus insurance details for his shattered windscreen, before I finally arrive all in one piece, at the bar. Publishing PR plebs introduce me to a loud American female acquaintance of theirs. She, like me, is a young and prominent writer. What's more she is clearly threatened by the competition and embarks upon a petty game of one-upmanship.

To make her feel less inferior I lie and play down my decidedly larger advance but still end up winning because it turns out that my book's being sold in Eire and hers isn't.

Saturday   **21 December**
                                          Katya's Birthday
Get up and check face for additional lines. Pleased to discover none that weren't there yesterday. Ring home to check my voice-mail for messages from well-wishers. Absolutely zilch – unless, of

course, a tirade of abuse from my washing man over the size of his Christmas bonus, and a curt reminder about my overdue *Fountain of Youth* subscription count as birthday greetings.

Thus, feeling mildly melancholy, arrive at my publisher's Christmas party at her house in the New Town. Sadly announce to all her guests that it is my birthday, thus stealing the show immediately. Publisher tactfully goes to bed early so I'm left to play surrogate host. Am disappointed to note no male talent save for a couple of DJs and actors passed their use-by date, a Swiss drug dealer called Claude and four members of an extremely youthful up-and-coming rock group.

Since the singer has brought his groupie along with him, and I refuse to be seen with a drummer or bassist hanging off my arm, let the lead guitarist trail behind me all night. However, am forced to rebuff his amorous advances later on the dance floor as I don't wish to be charged with corrupting a minor.

Leave party at two in the morning feeling even more depressed because everybody knows that attracting the attention of 15-year-olds is the first sign of old age.

Sunday   22 December
Tell accommodating British Airways staff that it's my birthday today and get upgraded to first class on my flight back to London. Can feel palpable air of sexual tension as I sashay down the aisle, so unused are rich businessmen to seeing a young woman at the front of the plane (most air stewardesses don't look a day under forty). By the end of my journey, I've been proffered eleven business cards but have only accepted three.

Monday   23 December
Ring and make New Year lunch-dates with two managing directors and a chairman of the board. Have no intention of showing up since I don't go out with men who try to procure young girls on planes. Nonetheless, enjoy the thought of keeping three rich and powerful men in a state of perpetual sexual frustration over the Christmas break.

Tuesday   **24 December**
                                                         Christmas Eve

Typical. Now that I'm finally free to pursue a hectic social life, all my friends are deserting me to spend Christmas with their families. I, of course, cannot impress anyone with my own strong family ties because my publisher has ordered that I not leave the town for the time being, saying she may want to bring me in for questioning about my manuscript.

   With nothing better to do, decide to do some serious shopping for people other than myself. Personally, I seem to get more joy out of receiving than giving but, not wishing to be outed by do-gooder Christian types, set off for Oxford Street with a list the length of my arm because I couldn't find any scrap paper to write it on. My magnanimity, which stretches from just above my wrist to just below my shoulder, includes make-up remover for Ferguson, a box of dates for Eliza, a mirror for Sophie, a book on sex education for Angel and a stain-free lipstick for Phoebe – the last time she locked lips with her married man she left Forever Amber on his collar. Don't know what I'm supposed to be buying for the likes of Carlotta, Biggles or my parents as I wrote their gift ideas in my armpit and I really don't feel like taking my top off in the middle of a busy street today.*

   After fruitless five hours wrestling with other shoppers, get home, lock door, close windows and draw curtains. Then take the phone off the hook and disconnect my telly in preparation for tomorrow when I am going to pretend that it is not Christmas Day . . .

See Saturday, 16 November.

Wednesday   **25 December**
                                                         Christmas Day

. . . cruelly reminded when I wake up and spot the usual disappointing assortment of bath salts, cookbooks and Chippendales calendars sitting under my giant cactus. Wallow in obligatory self-pity for a bit, then go to my fridge-freezer and open one of the more satisfactory bottle-shaped gifts I bought for myself.

   After successfully shunning all human contact for the next eight hours, start feeling unwanted and unloved. Seek reassurance by calling my mother in Barnsley, reverse charge. She tells me she can't talk long as she needs to keep her eye on the convicted criminal Carlotta has brought home for the holidays. Upon hearing he once held up a pizza-delivery boy at knife point, my mother is making the most of the silly season by hiding away all sharp objects (along with expensive ones like the stereo and video). Needless to say, the entire Livingston clan is presently on tenterhooks because Carlotta's erstwhile felon is now so sick of turkey and ham he's threatening to call Pizza Hut. After listening to this and other melodramas typical of my family, I now realise why I chose to spend Christmas Day in solitary confinement.

Thursday   **26 December**
                                                        Boxing Day

Open front door to let out vodka fumes and cigarette smoke, only to catch Ex hovering behind it with a glass beaker attached to his ear. Instinctively guess he's not here to borrow a cup of sugar because he knows I never keep food in the house.

It's a long time since I sprung him last. Indeed, once the restraining order expired, my one-time Romeo suddenly stopped doing romantic things like chasing after my car on foot or scaling drainpipes to reach my fourth-floor abode. Now it appears I've inadvertently lured him from his state of complacency through my bawdy column in *London Goss* and my recent exposé in a leading women's magazine, both of which tend to give the impression I'm having far more success with the opposite sex than he is. Do my best to massage his extremely delicate ego by declaring that all 28 of my most recent conquests meant nothing whatsoever. Then demand a Christmas present from him.

After handing over his dole cheque, Ex slopes off, apparently appeased.

Friday   **27 December**

Today I'm having a business meeting with party-plan consultant

Angel because I'm doing yet another newsletter for Jools & Co. Since the company is so happy with the work I've done to date (Die-monds to Die For!!!!!) and haven't baulked at the size of the invoice I sent them – mainly because they haven't seen it yet – I've decided to assert my rights and demand a business lunch. Unfortunately, still practising hard to become a suburban housewife, Angel's elected for Garfunkels in Brent Cross. Whilst I get heavily involved with the house whites, Angel bores me catatonic with pre-bridal banter, but I let her because she's picking up the bill.

Can't remember getting home. Or falling asleep fully-clothed.

Only roused out of my solid slumber by what sounds like a dirty old man heavy-breathing at the foot of my bed. Sadly, it just turns out to be a five-foot six-inch badger perspiring heavily on the edge of my balcony. Lean out of window and whack it with a vodka bottle I happen to have under my pillow.

Bottle and badger plummet into bushes six storeys below and I immediately get an attack of the guilts because the bottle was still half full. Thus waste a couple of hours rummaging through low-lying shrubs. Don't find my vodka or any injured mammal, though do spy Ex limping off into the sunset clad in a bedraggled black-and-white furry costume.

Saturday   **28 December**

Neighbours are starting to talk about the sudden rash of woodland creatures roaming the perimeter of my apartment.

'No pets allowed,' says one narky note pinned to my door.

'This is not a zoo,' another helpfully reminds me.

'Kindly remove that ridiculous-looking otter from my hallway,' beseeches a third.

Decide to resolve matters once and for all by confronting culprit who's now holed up in my stairwell posing as a giant rabbit, courtesy of the National Theatre's props department.

Threaten to marry it and have its babies if it doesn't desist from its animal theatrics. An all-too-familiar look of fear appears in Ex's eyes behind the bunny mask and he suddenly starts yabbering on about 'needing some space'. Tempted to tell him to go join NASA but, in a fit of feminine frustration, let fly with crockery instead whilst concerned tenants place calls to the RSPCA.

Sunday 29 December

The malcontents residing in my block seem determined not to peacefully co-exist with me. My landlady confirms this when she arrives unannounced after an anonymous tip-off.

My niggardly neighbours allege my smoke alarm goes off at annoyingly regular intervals (the stupid thing is super-sensitive to my occasional bouts of heavy smoking) and accuse me of airing my knickers on the balcony (this no doubt coming from the fatter female tenants who are jealous because I can actually fit into size-eight undies).

Almost manage to placate landlady, until she spots a particularly stubborn stain on the carpet that looks exactly like a burn from my ultra-steam iron, and then discovers I broke the waste-disposal unit trying to force-feed it with last year's telephone directories. I also don't think she was hugely impressed by the state of my balcony garden which I've deliberately transformed into an aesthetically pleasing, low-maintenance desert.

Monday 30 December

After a draining day trying to get my balcony reforestation project off the ground, feel like nice, refreshing bath. Whilst water's running, get distracted by rabid five-foot-six flying fox, complete with nylon brush tail, that is hanging precariously by its hands from a tree bough outside my bedroom window. By the time I've called in someone from the council's pest-control department (who in turn suggests I call out a psychiatric nurse), my entire flat is awash with water.

Once water levels are down, I wade into the living-room because unfortunately, now that I work from home, my desk-bound friends seem to think I have nothing better to do than risk electrocution and listen to their interminable woes on the phone all day.

Tuesday   **31 December**
New Year's Eve

More bothersome calls, including one from my landlady about my little flooding mishap yesterday. Apparently the ingrates who live below me arrived home from holiday today and got a bit upset – though I can't see why since at least they've had their carpets washed for free.

In afternoon, catch up with surgically enhanced and terminally insecure Ferguson at Comptons. With much wailing and gnashing of badly bonded new teeth, Ferguson says he suspects Adolf – who's been arriving late for his hourly massage each week – is having an affair. Frankly, I think my equine pal may be right since his recently acquired overbite makes him look like a horse. And not a particularly attractive one at that.

Since it's New Year's Eve, and Ferguson's gone to the men's room to scout for business, make hurried list of resolutions before I head off to Eliza's place in Camden for a night of rapacious revelry. Good intentions are, in the following order: quit getting rat-faced on tequila before midnight; quit kissing other inebriated revellers bang on midnight; quit luring best-looking kisser home after midnight thus avoiding having to kick him out during afterglow bit because he's useless in bed.

Get home late in afternoon, only to discover my door lock's been changed and my belongings thrown out into the street.

Wednesday   **1 January**
New Year's Day

Am lolling on a futon at Eliza's place in Camden, sipping her foul home-brewed ginger wine, quietly congratulating myself for achieving a personal best by breaking all my resolutions before 1. 03 a.m. and all the while empathising with displaced people the world over, I myself having just been uprooted from my place of abode because of cultural differences between me and my landlady.

Naturally, I've done everything I can to make myself feel at home at *chez* Eliza's but I still feel like a refugee. Eliza reckons I'm exaggerating. However, my once-accommodating friend certainly didn't act like a gracious host when the removal men dumped a lorry-load of my clothes in the middle of her living room yesterday afternoon, up-ending a wood-carved Balinese banana tree in the process. During the particularly graphic brawl that ensued between her and the hired help, I probably didn't help matters by agreeing with the latter that my cardboard boxes were a vast improvement on Eliza's ethnic monstrosities.

She also didn't seem too impressed when the man she'd set her sights on at last night's party wandered dazedly this morning out of the guest bedroom where I am currently sleeping. But, as I tried to reasonably explain to her, she should be grateful I saved him from the Curse of Namambo.

Thursday   **2 January**
After cooking me a decidedly sub-standard breakfast, Eliza ducks out of doing the dishes by sneaking off to work at my former place of employ. Grudgingly shove plates, cups and bowls into what I presume is the dishwasher, turn it on to 'High', and then make the most of free phone facilities by placing dozens of calls to let my friends know where I am – just in case they've been fretting or wish to invite me to stay once Eliza tires of me using all the hot water each morning.

No concrete offers today, although Teddington did volunteer some space at his place in Kentish Town as there's quite a bit of it now that his muse has left him. Needless to say, I had to knock him back. One of my lifelong dreams is to avoid living in a warehouse that has yet to be renovated.

Friday   **3 January**
A tight-lipped Eliza invades my room at six in the morning carrying a breakfast tray laden down with non-recyclable plastic plates and an extra-early edition of *Loot*. Since she's civil enough not to mention the fact I blew up an entire 24-piece bone china dinner set in her fan-assisted oven yesterday, humour her by circling a few accommodation classifieds with a pen.

Leave the paper in a prominent and reassuring position by the phone and sneak out for slightly less awful feed at Wendy's in Wimbledon, compliments of pregnant party-planner, Angel. Clad in a maternity smock from Littlewoods and dripping in her company's not even semi-precious stones, she's called this business meeting to inform me that Jools & Co can no longer afford my freelance copywriting rates, nor indeed my demand for 'expensive' client lunches.

Since I refuse Angel's generous counter-offer (payment in the form of non-hypoallergenic trinkets), I formally hand in my notice, and then get down to more important matters – like how to dissuade Angel from committing further social suicide by marrying Bogie Boy.

Sure enough, with a little prompting from me, Angel reveals there's trouble in paradise. Indeed, she caught her cheapskate fiancé buying her wedding ring in the January sales. To be perfectly honest, I'm surprised he didn't get it out of the Jools & Co winter catalogue.

Despite my protests to the contrary, Angel seems determined to go ahead with wedding plans, proclaiming she wants her child to have a father – even if it is one who thinks Donna Karan is a Lebanese fast food.

Saturday   **4 January**
Room temperature is -2°C and too cold to do anything but swelter in a public bath-house sauna in W2 with sun-sycophant Ferguson. Am therefore huddled under a large towel, checking out other people's cellulite. Ferguson is oblivious to my discomfort because he's too busy prattling on about his new new-age 'boyfriend' Forest. In exchange for a relationship of sorts, Ferguson confides he's committed himself to cleaning Forest's apartment once a week for free. Sadly, even the thought of my foppish friend prancing around in a French maid's outfit and flaunting a feather duster does nothing to improve my mood.

Emerge frazzled and wan from the sauna five hours later and, worse still, receive not a cursory glance from the golden-skinned gods parading poolside. Upon seeing my panic-stricken white face and conveniently forgetting the fact he's spent the last two weeks welded to a solarium lamp, Ferguson tries to console me by saying 'pale and interesting' is all the rage. Ignore his asinine attempts at flattery and pick up a tube of fake tanning cream on my way back to Eliza's place.

Sunday   5 January

Two knocks on door. Refuse to answer. Eliza's morning paper arrives. Sneak out to get it.

This is all because I am covered from head to toe in unsightly orange streaks. For most of the day, I lie on top of Eliza's unbleached calico, bronze-stained bed sheets cursing myself for not reading the instructions on the tube properly.

By evening, it's still too cold to do anything but make myself feel warmer by watching the Australian Tennis Open on the telly and wonder why opponents waste their energies chasing the ball. As far as I'm concerned, they'd all be much better off standing stock-still on the scorching centre court to see who collapses first.

Meantime, Eliza gets under my feet mopping, dusting and cooking, irritating me beyond belief.

Monday   6 January

Fake tan less virulent, so venture outdoors again in bid to avoid the revolting lunch Eliza's left on the kitchen bench.

Make my first-ever concession to my lifetime ban on sitting in no-smoking zones and brave children's matinee film session at a fully heated Virgin cinema on Fulham Road.

When movies for the grown-ups start, discover all the good ones are sold out so have to leave my warm confines because I'd rather die from hypothermia than endure two hours of Kevin Costner.

Tuesday   7 January

Even cooler change on weather and home front. Eliza has left a passive-aggressive note on her fridge door to say that if I wish to be fed again I'd better pick up some groceries.

This is the last straw. If she thinks I'm putting up with her reprehensible cooking a minute longer, she deserves to be abandoned.

Call my mother in Barnsley and tell her I'm coming to stay with her and my father until I get back on my feet again. Then ring Teddington and demand he pay for my first-class train fare because I know for a fact he gets paid cash in hand. Grateful to hear that I'm not going to report his undeclared earnings to the DSS, Teddington is more than happy to help me out.

Wednesday   8 January
Am currently crouched over a toilet bowl in Yorkshire, ruing the day I was born. Having clearly not forgiven me for turning them back at King's Cross station last year, my parents seem determined to make my enforced stay in 'the north' as miserable as possible.

Ever since the time my mother accidentally ran over a Hereford cow on the high street, my parents have been died-in-the-wool vegans and so I have been duly greeted with great bowls of vile green sludge posing as breakfast, lunch and dinner. If I didn't know better I would suggest I was being force-fed grass cuttings. But, given that my father mows lawns for a living, I've been keeping an eye on compost bin levels.

Worse still, my mother has converted my childhood bedroom into a conservatory, so I have to make do with my parents' lumpen queen-size bed whilst they sleep in the garden shed. If this isn't bad enough, I have also been told that I've got to smoke outside in the bitter cold because my father is asthmatic.

Like I tell him, at this rate am afraid I will regress into a spoilt and petulant child very quickly. My father doesn't appear too perturbed to hear this and says I've never been anything but.

Stomp off to their bedroom without giving either of them a kiss goodnight.

Thursday   9 January
At six in the morning, my mother bangs on her bedroom door and asks me if I've got any laundry that needs doing. Point to the full

complement of Louis Vuitton luggage at my bedside, then fall back into slumber.

Wake up at around noon and clamber out of bed. For want of anything better to do in the sticks, trail after my mother who takes me sightseeing at a nearby village because she needs to stock up on lima beans and muesli since the bags in her cupboard went mysteriously missing last night.

At some ye olde people's café, order a latte and am met with a blank-eyed stare from the waitress. Decide not to complicate things any further, so ask for a Fanta instead. Determined to stretch our fragile mother-daughter bond to breaking point, Ma Livingston then tries to make conversation by asking me about my non-existent love life. Tempted to chuck a tantrum right then and there but don't because the locals have already started gathering around our table to gawk at my designer clothes.

Things don't get much better come evening when I spend the night at some grotty pub in the rough part of Barnsley with Carlotta, who now lives away from home at the request of my parents. Having ditched the convicted criminal she was recently dating for stealing her railcard, she is now, unfortunately, footloose and fancy-free. This means I am subjected to another episode of her outrageous mating rituals which tend to involve staring at the most obvious undesirable in the room until he feels obliged to come over and buy her some drinks.

I feel out of my depth amongst such unpedigreed people but as a matter of principle and petty sibling rivalry am forced to compete. I must say, the two hairy cretins from the Death's Head biker gang don't need much encouragement.

Friday   **10 January**
Pictures from the moon today will capture a long-suffering, horrendously hung over city girl (who will never, ever, *ever* again drink a full bottle of rum and then try to make out on a Harley) reclining on a cement bag, smoking a Marlboro and watching her mother attempt to build the second Great Wall of Yorkshire. My parents' house sits on a reclaimed slag heap so naturally my

mother has taken it upon herself to landscape half an acre of rough terrain with hand-hewn stone.

Finally get tired of watching her mix up 50 kilos of concrete and heave 12 five-tonne rocks uphill, so go back indoors again and call all my friends in London to see if anyone cares to rescue me from my self-imposed exile.

As luck would have it, full-time heiress and professional husband-hunter, Frangipani, says she's got to dash off to Hong Kong in order to suck up to a rich but seriously ailing relative, which means I get to house-sit a heavily mortgaged Primrose Hill mansion for a while. Unfortunately, Frangipani says I can't move in until she's moved out which means I've got three more days of torture to go.

To be honest, I'm quite surprised at Frangipani's magnanimous gesture. We last spoke eight months ago, at which time dialogue halted abruptly after Frangipani broke off her engagement to a millionaire stockbroker because she assumed, quite correctly as it happens, that he secretly fancied me.

Saturday   **11 January**
Determined to avoid another hard day's slog down the trenches, borrow my mother's second-hand Escort and drive into Sheffield. This turns out to be a fairly harrowing journey since my mode of transport is completely lacking in optional extras like wheel alignment, suspension, brake pads and rear-view mirror. Seeing as it's really the country I don't bother locking the car doors when I arrive in the city centre. Besides, I'm not used to cars without central locking.

Spend best part of day hiding behind racks of clothes in the Meadowhall shopping centre because Sheffield is a very small place and I spot at least a dozen disgruntled exes whose hearts I broke into smithereens when I was but a teenage temptress. When I finally get back to the car, discover it's not there any more.

My mother doesn't take the news exceedingly well, despite the fact I pointed out to her that there's a perfectly good ride-on lawnmower in the garden shed.

Sunday   **12 January**

Police ring to say they've found my mother's Escort. After having to push it through six sets of red lights and three stop signs, the joyriders who stole it eventually abandoned it outside a scrap yard in Sheffield.

To celebrate, we have a pot roast at home. Luckily, the same thief who snaffled the lima beans and muesli also made off with the nutmeat so my mother reluctantly concedes to my suggestion we eat proper food for a change. Of course, she has to briefly look away when I unthinkingly toss a rump steak on to the woodstove.

Monday   **13 January**

Last few hours of cultural deprivation.

At Barnsley station, my mother tearfully hands me a cheap and nasty key ring shaped like a pithead as a souvenir of my stay. As soon as my parents head for the station exit, dump my unwanted gift into an unsuspecting passenger's backpack.

Tuesday   **14 January**

Arrive back in London and head straight for Frangipani's Edwardian pile in Primrose Hill. Am not a massive fan of lawnmower land but it's better than bunking up at Eliza's self-styled ashram in Camden or my parents' Calvinist cottage in Barnsley.

Ever the philanthropist, Frangipani isn't charging me any rent, instead saying she's glad to do her bit for the homeless. Privately, I think her kindly gesture has got more to do with the fact she needs someone to feed Leicester, the extremely rare and expensive Chinese bulldog I've just found lurking behind the front door.

Frangipani has also asked that I use the wads of cash she's left on the kitchen bench to pay for her Macedonian cleaner and Chinese gardener – the latter in particular seeming to me like an unnecessary extravagance since I intend to neither paddle in the Olympic-size pool nor frolic across the manicured lawns.

Immediately sack the gardener and send him packing off back to Immigration. The cleaner gets a last-minute reprieve, however. She's so impressed to be slaving for a celebrity columnist (and soon-to-be-published author), she's agreed to do all domestic duties for half the price in future.

Wednesday   15 January
Spend enjoyable morning rattling around ten bedrooms, four bathrooms, two kitchens and a ballroom, pillaging drawers and shuffling through shelves trying to work out the net worth of my absent friend.

At six million pounds, and still counting, realise how poor I am so drive to McDonald's to get some lunch. Imagine my immense revulsion but complete lack of surprise at finding my old advertising foe, Sebastian, twitching nervously behind the counter. Both of us being mature, sensible adults, he refrains from spitting on my Chicken McNuggets and I try not to snigger too loudly at his hairnet. Instead, we talk about common interests like how I'm a huge commercial success and he's not.

Then, in a blatant attempt at bribery and corruption, he slips me an extra sachet of mustard sauce, so I return the favour and pass him the name of three advertising agencies that I know for a fact aren't hiring anybody in the near future.

Thursday   16 January
Have not had much sleep of late as I am now with dog. Would prefer to be without, but this is impossible as Leicester's mistress obviously guessed I might try to shirk my dog-sitting duties and has accordingly instructed the local animal shelter not to take him off my hands.

Putting up with a fat, useless pug that breaks wind in bed and steals the covers is a small price to pay for living rent-free in Frangipani's sprawling estate but, as I tried to tell the unco-operative shelter person today, I refuse to let any male lie prostrate on top of me in the middle of the night, snoring loudly in my ear, unless he buys me a ring first.

Friday   17 January
Check Frangipani's letter box to see if the Royal Mail really is

capable of complicated tasks like redirecting my post, and am greeted with a positively vitriolic note from Calliope saying she's finally escaped from Algeria, is heading for the US and thanks very much for omitting to notify the British Embassy about her terrifying kidnapping ordeal.

This is an unfair accusation considering I didn't realise her last, extremely cryptic postcard was a cry for help, since words like 'prisoner', 'ransom' and 'appalling food' had been inked out by Middle Eastern postal services.

Next bout of abuse comes when I ring my foolhardy agent to find out how my book is going. At risk of losing her percentage of my future endeavours, she gently chides me for disappearing off the face of the earth.

Apparently, a fortnight's a long time in publishing and in my absence she's had to make a number of 'executive decisions' on my behalf. These include: agreeing with the designer that the book's title should be larger than the author's name; agreeing with the editor that some of my more enterprising and highly imaginative sex scenes be deleted; and agreeing with the publisher that I am indeed possibly the most difficult author she has ever had the misfortune to work with.

What do they expect, I think savagely to myself as I slam down the phone and hurl it through a pane of the French windows. Anyone creative is bound to be a little bit temperamental.

Saturday   **18 January**

Am stuck behind enemy lines in the middle of nowhere, cursing myself for getting roped into stupid war games with Sebastian and his trigger-happy friends.

I naively thought my invitation was Sebastian's rather indirect way of calling a truce. He called me early this morning to thank me for the advertising leads I gave him the other day. Then he asked if I'd like to 'make up numbers' in a 'friendly game of paintball warfare'. Whilst I have no intention of grasping any olive branch that Sebastian cares to extend, I did think that it might be a good opportunity to meet a few men who aren't intimidated by a strong woman.

Started having some serious doubts about Sebastian's supposed *détente* when I learnt he was going to be on the opposing team. Needless to say, I played it safe and shot him execution-style before the game began whilst he was still struggling into his bullet-proof overalls. As soon as he was airlifted to the hospital, all hell broke loose and now his pathological pals have started gunning for me big time.

Arrive back at Frangipani's place late in the afternoon, battered and bruised, and dismayed to discover that Leicester is clearly a bit peeved that I haven't got round to taking him for a walk yet. Indeed, it appears my malevolent mutt has dug holes in Frangipani's immaculate lawns and thoroughly trounced her previously well-tended flowerbeds.

Sunday   **19 January**
Have just tethered Leicester to an antique wrought-iron hatstand as punishment for slobbering over the Manolo Blahnik sandals I bought for myself at Christmas (since no one else bothered to). At my wit's end, ring Teddington for some house-training tips as he's the only friend of mine who's come even remotely close to owning a pet, having once had rats in his Kentish Town warehouse. Subsequently shocked to hear his ex-muse at the other end of the line. She coolly tells me he's laid up in hospital after pranging his paraglider into a particularly unyielding cliff-face in Dover recently. Since Teddington has never been the athletic type, I presume his latest act of lunacy was a last-ditch attempt to win old sourpuss back by pretending he was a real man instead of a New Age sensitive one.

Did feel a momentary pang of conscience for vehemently refusing to go visit him but the thought of listening to Teddington have a legitimate reason to whinge is more than I can bear. Anyway, he's probably in the same ward as Sebastian and I hear the latter's family is holding a particularly overwrought bedside vigil and I'd really prefer not to walk into a potential scene from *The Godfather.*

Monday   **20 January**
Get up bright and early to catch the morning rush-hour traffic.
Push Leicester out of the house. Lob tennis ball out on to main
road and absent-mindedly leave the front gate open.

Tuesday   **21 January**
Not content with causing a five-car pile-up outside Frangipani's
house yesterday morning, Leicester chewed the leg off one of her
fifteenth-century 12-seater dinner tables and, worse still, tried to
attack me after I whacked him over the head with his Wedgwood
china dog bowl (which wasn't that heavy anyway as there was no
food in it because I'd forgotten to buy any).

    Hopefully, some sympathetic vet will come around to my way of
thinking and I will be put out of my misery at last.

Wednesday   **22 January**
No luck with vets, so mistakenly cut off Leicester's ID tags and
accidentally lose him outside a pet shop in Archway on the long-
way round to lunch with Phoebe in King's Cross.

    It's been a long time between courses and I must say I hardly
recognise her, clad as she is in platinum-blonde wig, PVC mini and
thigh-high boots. So bitterly disillusioned is old Phoebe about
being the other woman for the best part of a decade, she's decided
that if she's going to sleep with married men she might as well get
paid for it.

    We trade techniques and work out that if I charged for all the
services I'd rendered to manhood I'd be rich enough to lure a gold-
digging toyboy as opposed to the penniless old codgers I generally
tend to attract.

Thursday   **23 January**
Talking of which, today I receive a nuisance call from the ex who,
in a rather drastic attempt to stop himself from stalking me and
in a pathetic attempt to get a paid speaking role, has fled to Alice
Springs in Australia and is now a tour guide on one of those 18-
to-35 package tours (though how he qualified is completely

beyond me since he's not a day under 40 and has the paunch to prove it).

However, for obvious sentimental reasons, he still likes to occasionally ring me from his mobile then hang up when I answer – no doubt checking to see that I'm not swanning around with other men.

Friday   **24 January**
Under extreme sufferance, and only because I'm feeling sanguine because he's recently had a horrifically traumatising spleen transplant thanks to rupturing his in the paragliding prang, agree to join Teddington at an Angus Steakhouse on Oxford Street.

Ignoring the sounds of mooing emanating from the kitchen, as well as the disgusting sight of Teddington hawking bits of horn and hoof on to his side plate, I spit blood at the waiter who misinterpreted my 'medium rare' for 'still palpably breathing'. Ignoring Teddington's mindless whimperings about how his muse wasn't won over by his mid-air heroics, drag him to the aptly named Crown of Thorns so that he can buy me a more palatable iron supplement. Once there, get harassed by an American tourist who foolishly thinks I'll shout him a pint of Guinness just because he mistakes me for Cameron Diaz.

Saturday   **25 January**
Rouse myself out of bed at a reasonable hour as I have to go to church, though it is only because Angel is getting married. Having successfully avoided her emergency engagement party, hurried hen's night and quick kitchen tea, I'd prefer to also skip the shotgun wedding and rather hastily booked reception at the back of a Chinese restaurant in Wood Green. But think better of it as I am the head bridesmaid and Angel needs at least one photogenic member in her bridal party, if just for some decent wedding snaps.

Things don't get off to a good start at the church, especially when Angel's dad springs the groom bolting the wrong way down the aisle. At the end of a decidedly monotonous and highly strung ceremony, Angel bursts into racking sobs, though I think it has little to do with the romance of the occasion and more to do with the fact she caught her reluctant spouse eyeing me in a covetous way during the marital vows.

Am not particularly popular with the bridesmaids either since I caught the bouquet. I must admit, this wasn't terribly hard to do since I was clad only in short stretch Lycra whilst they all rushed futiley forth in full Elizabethan regalia.

Sunday   26 January
Receive another nuisance call from Ex who's still entertaining back-packers in Alice Springs. This time, though, I think his call is accidental as he doesn't seem to have a clue that I'm on the other end of the line. He must have inadvertently hit the 'redial' button on his mobile and thus I have to endure hearing him huff and puff his way up Ayers Rock for two and a half hours before his phone battery finally goes flat.

Would have preferred not to listen in on what is clearly a very gruelling and potentially fatal climb for a man in his condition, but refuse to hang up as he's on a low-payment mobile phone plan and the call will hopefully be costing him at least one hundred pounds a minute.

Monday   27 January
Typical. Having just bought my first batch of groceries for the new year, I've had to throw the lot out because an article I've just read in a women's magazine says packaged goods may contain preservatives which cause premature ageing.

Now it looks like I'm going to have to resort to fresh fruit and vegetables or, worse still, dog food (which has been going to waste in the pantry ever since I lost my four-legged friend, Leicester, so tragically six days ago).

Tuesday   28 January
After a definitively disgusting meal of Lassie Rabbit Chunks, have to make an emergency stop-over at Gatwick Airport to collect a

heavily pregnant and completely hysterical Angel who has cut short her honeymoon in Tossa del Mar, no doubt because she caught her dearly beloved engaged in the perverted act of buying – and then wearing – locally produced T-shirts.

After just three days and two nights of marital bliss, Angel's already talking divorce, tearfully telling me she thinks that Bogie Boy may not be husband material, after all. Tempted to tell her she should have realised all this when he insisted upon taking her to Segaworld on their first date.

However, desist from any cheap shots about him in her hour of need and instead make appropriate soothing sounds, drop her off at her flat in Tottenham and promise that I'll always be there for her and baby-to-be, knowing full well she and Bogie Boy will probably be back together again by week's end.

Wednesday   29 January
Tried the optimistically termed Good-O Doggie Delites today. Now I know why Leicester used to pad about the house with such a hangdog look on his face.

Thursday   30 January
Wake up in panic-stricken state because, according to some spiteful current affairs programme I watched last night, I've got less than five years left before my social life is reduced to a pathetic whirl of male-escort services, desperate and dateless balls and cats – all of which I am severely allergic too.

Head straight for Doctor Love's surgery to tell him I've got women's problems. Misunderstanding my self-diagnosis completely, my debonair doctor reaches for his rubber gloves and surgical steel probe, which I tell him will be a fat lot of help since I'm not talking about *those* kinds of women's problems. I am, in fact, suffering from involuntary sexual repression and associated psychosomatic disorders due to the fact I haven't banged headboards with a member of the opposite sex in quite some time.

Have a feeling Doctor Love would have willingly volunteered to oblige me then and there, but holds himself in check admirably and instead gives me the name of an eminent psychologist in Bloomsbury.

After I'm assured said shrink is male, divorced and easy to talk to, leave surgery feeling slightly less depressed because at least now I'll have someone to practise my feminine wiles on.

Friday   31 January
Am absolutely furious. Have just frittered away hundreds of pounds, only to be told by some smug professorial type that the reason I can't get a man is because I am *self-absorbed* and *self-obsessed*. Like I said to him in somewhat steely tones after my six-and-a-half-hour session was up, why else would I need to see a shrink?

Decide to get a second male opinion, so call my brother, Biggles, who is still flying crop-sprayers in Senegal. When I finally pause for breath, Biggles reluctantly admits that I do have a habit of monopolising conversations and that he has the reverse-charge, long-distance telephone bills to prove it.

Saturday   1 February
Resolve to turn over a new leaf until I reel in my Romeo. Consequently, vamp down to Café de Paris, swoop down upon the first male who looks at me sidewards, hold my tongue and let him talk about himself instead.

End up falling asleep at the bar.

Sunday   2 February
Decide to go pour out my lovelorn woes to Teddington at the Coach & Horses.

Teddington decants a generous measure of top-shelf Absolut into a pint glass for me and then, before I've even opened my mouth to speak, says he was wondering if I could use my *London Goss* column to air his petty gripes. Since I've made it a policy to never publicise social injustices of any kind lest I appear biased, I almost choke on my drink, so desperate am I to finish it all before I have to break the bad news to him and risk having the glass ripped out from my hand.

Mercifully, Teddington is a painfully slow talker and dreadfully long-winded storyteller, so I've managed to guzzle my drink and knock back a few more before he's finished explaining the whole sorry affair. Bang my sixth empty spirit-stained beer glass down on the counter and abruptly tell him I've got better things to do with my time than listen to him prattle on about his problems with his private medical insurance company. And besides, I add as a parting shot, I'm glad to hear that he is about to embark upon a long and noble legal battle with them as I presume it means he won't have time to write any more bad prose for a while.

Monday   3 February
Too hung over to move, let alone go out and quietly chat up men.

Tuesday   4 February
In evening, accompany a spangled and feathered Ferguson to a desperate and dateless ball disguised as a ballroom-dancing competition near Piccadilly Circus. Am only going because he's without a partner as usual. (Forest, his New Age ex-boyfriend, cancelled his saucy French-maid sessions after Ferguson accidentally touched his precious healing crystals whilst dusting the mantelpiece.)

As soon as we arrive at the hall, fob Ferguson off with another dancing queen and head straight for the hetero horrors in the corner. There's not a lot to choose from, I must admit, but put my best foot forward and yank one with the most dandruff on to the dance floor. Unaware about things like women's rights and girl power, my would-be waltzing partner keeps trying to take the lead. A small battle of wills ensues and he ends up flat on his back on the floor and – tragically for him – without me following in hot pursuit.

Wednesday   5 February
Am currently assuming the lotus position in a Camden warehouse and casting withering glances at Eliza who told me this is a good

place to meet members of the opposite sex. I should have known that the kind of man who does yoga is hardly the sort to throw me over the bonnet of his BMW and ravish me to death before handing over his well-stuffed wallet. Furthermore, I fail to see how sitting on a cold hardwood floor risking haemorrhoids and hernias whilst saying 'Om' a lot is meant to make me feel relaxed.

Thursday   6 February
In yet another drastic attempt to avoid impending spinsterhood, head off to some workers' pub in Stepney with happy hooker Phoebe. She's managed to convince me that since it's one of those old-fashioned men-only hang-outs, we'll no doubt have to beat suitors off with my Prada bag. Granted, whilst our entrance is greeted with a gob-smacked silence which I would like to think was in awe and admiration, I fear it's probably because they've never seen a woman dressed in natural fibres before. Either that, or it's the sight of Phoebe who never goes anywhere these days without her zippered black mask and cat o' nine tails.

Phoebe and I quaff shandies (since our requests for Banana Daiquiris were met with a dull-eyed stare from the barman) and the men resume their conversation. When one of them starts cursing and carrying on, he promptly gets kicked out by the other patrons who loudly remind him that there are 'ladies' in the house. Whilst it's nice to see that chivalry isn't dead in the outer suburbs, I object to being referred to as a 'lady' because it's so blatantly ageist.

Friday   7 February
Armed with a five-gallon drum of Liquid Paper, spend entire day falsifying my year of birth on my driving licence, passport and birth certificate.

Counterfeiting process interrupted when one of Frangipani's seven phones ring. It's my personal patron of the arts herself calling to say she's coming home earlier than expected because having to grease up to her blue-blooded relatives in Hong Kong is too high a price to pay for getting her hands on the family trust.

This news puts me in a mild state of panic, to say the least. I may have to do a premature moonlight flit from her palatial premises for I believe her wrath will know no limits when she discovers I've fired the family gardener, am considering poaching her Macedonian cleaner and have misplaced Leicester, a bulldog so pedigreed it was used as collateral on the house.

Saturday   8 February
Given that my love life is being seriously hampered by document falsification endeavours, I'm tempted to turn my much revered *London Goss* column into my very own personal dating service. Unfortunately, the sort of male hopefuls who put pen to paper to me tend to err on the side of mad or desperate – though I cannot for the life of me work out why since I sanitise my life for the column.

Only suitable suitor this week is Frank of Finchley who writes to say he's a 70-year-old pensioner who forgoes his weekly packet of McVitie's Chocolate Homewheats just so as he can afford to purchase *London Goss* and read about my youthful tales of derring-do.

Write firm but friendly note back to him saying that unless he looks like Sean Connery, or has a seven-figure life-assurance policy, I'm not particularly interested.

Sunday   9 February
Start manhunt early today. Head off to Hyde Park, set up elaborate trip-wire and wait for some out-of-condition businessman in jogging shorts to fall at my feet and thus be forced to get to know me better. After collecting only two old ladies and a poodle, get disheartened and go back home again.

Monday   10 February
Still determined to make the most of my relatively short use-by date as a not-quite-yet-on-the-shelf female and find myself another man. Of course, meeting up for drinks at Black Cat with my pal Sophie, who has no interest in the opposite sex whatsoever, only serves to exacerbate my sense of urgency.

Let her bang on about being a lonely lesbian for as long as is politely possible without lapsing into a coma. Then rudely cutting her off by saying I don't see what she's got to worry about since, if statistics are true, there must be plenty of needy single women over the age of 35 for her to choose from.

Tuesday   **11 February**
Self-esteem hits an all-time low today.

The once-obsessive ex showed up this morning with nary a stealthy pose nor a piece of surveillance equipment in sight. Instead, he stood as proud and as tall and as fearless as any grown man can when clad only in leather chaps and a dog collar. From what I could gather – and I must admit I didn't quite catch everything he said since his words were muffled through the recently acquired handlebar moustache – thanks to a spot of male-bonding that got out of hand in Australia's Northern Territory recently, he'll be leaping out of closets rather than bushes in future. This renders the new restraining order I've just had drawn up obsolete and will no doubt make me an object of monumental pity rather than insurmountable desire amongst my burgeoning circle of male admirers.

Thankfully, Ex promised me his new-found leanings have nothing whatsoever to do with the trauma of dating me for four years and everything to do with the fact he was forced to watch Hollywood musicals as a child.

After he skips gaily off into the sunset, I ring Ferguson for some emergency counselling but old Ferguson just callously asks for his phone number.

Wednesday   **12 February**
In a futile attempt to cheer myself up today, visit bookshops on Charing Cross Road and envisage *3½ Minutes* on all their shelves next month. Complete waste of time.

Thursday   **13 February**
Despondency develops into fully blown depression after Angel waddles unannounced into my Primrose Hill digs, waggles divorce

application forms in front of my face, and says that since I've played such a big part in convincing her to give Bogie Boy the boot, she expects me to take his place in the delivery room when the big day arrives.

Friday   **14 February**
                                                           Valentine's Day
Absolutely pathetic crop this year. One thinly veiled death threat disguised as a wreath from Sebastian, who obviously still hasn't had the good grace to forgive me for my little shooting mishap last month, plus a single red rose on the windscreen of my car. Unfortunately, I have yet to meet a secret admirer who I've actually ever fancied, so it is with a certain grim resolve that I unfurl a roll of barbed wire the length of the windscreen along with a note saying: *Leave dead plants here at own risk.*

Later, whilst preparing for a night on the prowl with fellow desperate Eliza, my rootless pal Calliope calls from her new temporary home at a YWCA in New York to say that after pit stops in Asia, the Middle East and Europe, she still hasn't found anyone who'll sleep with her.

This is depressing news. If she can't get the least bit ravished whilst traversing half the globe, there's fat chance of me getting lucky trolling up and down King's Road.

Saturday   **15 February**
Kick virile young barman out of bed in late afternoon as I have to do lunch at less-than-expensive Soho restaurant courtesy of my ex-boss who is trying to lure me back to the ad agency because my replacement, the Gatekeeper, is starting to act just like a proper advertising creative by demanding ridiculous amounts of money.

Am appalled to learn that the dining area is no-smoking and patrons can only puff at the bar. Pick up my plate and ciggies and plonk myself on a bar stool at the front of the restaurant, leaving my former employer to eat by himself at a table-for-two down the back. Our long-distance lunch is punctuated only by multiple ten-digit hand signals from him indicating the amounts he's willing to squander on my writing talents, followed by two-fingered ones from me indicating what he can do with such offensively low offers.

Sunday   16 February

After arriving back from Hong Kong only to find her Primrose Hill mansion in a state of wanton dishevelment and me, the house-sitter, trying to get Liquid Paper stains out of an antique lacquered desk with my finger nails, my personal benefactor Frangipani has kindly volunteered to put me up at the Hilton for a month whilst I look for another place to live. She's in an extra-charitable mood because, although her disgustingly rich great-aunt Amelia didn't shuffle off the mortal coil as anticipated, Frangipani did manage to meet an eligible merchant banker during her short stay. What's more, she smugly informs me, he owns three jewellery outlets in London *and* an island resort off Queensland.

Upon hearing this, would like to have stood my ground and held out for the more five-star Dorchester, but wisely don't for I have a feeling that as soon as Frangipani finds out that Leicester isn't really at the local dog-grooming salon having another facelift, her generous offer could well be reduced to three nights at a women's refuge in Streatham.

Monday   17 February

Wake up to discover Frangipani has thoughtfully packed my suitcase and booked me a minicab to the hotel.

My room there is a trifle on the pokey side but thankfully the minibar is deep and spacious. I think the porter is somewhat startled when I immediately begin leaping up and down on the bed in order to check the spring suspension – just in case I get any nocturnal visitors of the male variety.

Tuesday   18 February

Open my eyes late morning and hear Eliza gently snoring beside me. For one horrendous moment I think I must have succumbed to fleshly pleasures of the alternative kind, though all I can remember is her lobbing up to my room last night and encouraging me to open four £100 bottles of French champagne, no doubt to try and get her own back for me drinking all hers after I'd demolished her foul home-made ginger wine while I stayed last month. Mercifully though, when Eliza finally wakes up she doesn't gaze at me in that all-too-familiar, adoring way and ask me for my hand in marriage. So I figure nothing happened.

In the afternoon, more parasitic friends (Ferguson, Phoebe and Angel) come out of the woodwork in order to raid my minibar and take advantage of my room-service tab in the futile hope that I'll foot the bill. On their way out, make each of them hand over fifty quid and incur myself a substantial profit as I'm charging it all to Frangipani's Amex.

Wednesday   19 February
Spend morning in hotel bed channel surfing and accidentally hit the adult movie button and catch the diminutive John Wayne Bobbit in the act, post-snip. Can't work out why he bothered with all that extensive microsurgery since no woman would have been any the wiser if he hadn't.

Thursday   20 February
Mr Bobbit's lacklustre performance yesterday reminds me today that some of us are much less fortunate than others. Conscience thus pricked, decide to invite some nearby homeless kids back to my hotel room for a decent feed and a stern lecture on family values.

I must say, my bountiful gestures are met with extremely bad grace. The brats turn their noses up at the grilled sea bass, refuse to drink their Cokes unless they're watered down with Jack Daniels miniatures. To top it all off, they then try to make off with the towels, the bathrobes, the bed linen, the pillows, the mattress, the iron, the hairdryer, the television plus all the other things I've earmarked for my own possession when I finally vacate.

Friday   **21 February**

After breakfast in bed for five mornings in a row, have decided luxury living is getting decidedly tedious. A good thing too really, given I've just received a terse fax from Frangipani telling me that the party's over and, in a fit of unprecedented spite and malice, she has just put a stop on her credit card. I have a feeling she may have found out the truth about Leicester.

Am thus forced out on to the street-level lobby whilst I wait for the valet boy to collect my Honda Civic hatchback. When I ring numerous other 'friends' reverse-charge from my car mobile, many refuse to take my call whilst others flatly turn down my generous offer to keep them company for a few months until I can find alternative digs. The only people I don't bother phoning are Sophie (because I don't want men getting the wrong idea) and soon-to-be single mother Angel (because I suspect she'll leap at the chance of securing a live-in nanny).

Saturday   **22 February**

Wake up on Fulham Broadway at five past eight in the morning with stiff neck and cramp in my legs, only to spy a traffic warden leering at me through my car windscreen and planting a parking ticket under my wipers because I am parked on a crosswalk outside an estate agent's office. Worse still, when I check the rental property list, the only flat worth inhabiting is not open for inspection until tomorrow.

Swallow my pride, drive to Kentish Town and loiter pathetically outside Teddington's warehouse. He finally takes pity on me and my tragic plight and says I can stay the night if I read the first couple of chapters of his latest unpublishable piece.

Decide to down a bottle of Doctor Love's sedatives instead and sleep in my temporary mobile home in a nearby side street.

Sunday   **23 February**

Slept through my car alarm last night and was consequently burgled. All my compact discs (except Mariah Carey, Celine Dion and the Lighthouse Family) are missing. When I stumble out of the car and on to the pavement, I find my hub caps have also disappeared. Then, because of my slightly wild and unkempt state, I get propositioned by a kerb-crawling creep who mistakes me for a lady of ill-repute.

Drive straight over to Eliza's place in Camden to have a bath and press my clothes. She reluctantly shows me the bathroom door and studiously ignores my loud hints about how unfair it is that someone as statuesque as myself has to sleep in the cramped quarters of a Honda Civic hatchback. When I leave, she starts feeling badly about being such an unsympathetic cow, and hands me some pre-moistened towelettes plus a portable iron that plugs straight into the car lighter.

Rendezvous with my rental property manager at the studio apartment in Kensington and am told I can move in on Tuesday – providing I can supply at least one glowing reference.

As a last resort, give her the name of an estate agent who I once allowed to sleep with me during my less discerning days.

Monday   **24 February**

Following an appalling night's sleep in a spectacularly noisy 24-hour drive-in McDonald's carpark, my wake-up call is provided by some delinquent teen trying to dispose of his Egg McMuffin wrappers through my slightly open driver's seat window. Never in the best of moods first thing in the morning, I soon have him howling in agony. When he finally promises to hand over enough money for a couple of hash browns and strong cup of coffee, I release the 'window up' button and set his fingers free.

After all this drama, and all before seven o'clock in the morning, decide to move straight on to Notting Hill because I'm supposed to be meeting Sophie at the Earl of Londsdale at eight o'clock this evening and getting a car space off Portobello Road is always hell. By nightfall, I've managed to find a no-parking spot down one of those poky little streets that all look the same in the dark – particularly under the influence of 12 Bloody Marys.

Once at the bar and without so much as batting an unmade eyelid, Sophie, my fickle friend, sorrowfully informs me that because she can't have the woman of her dreams, she's decided to cross enemy lines and try out a member of the opposite sex.

Am not greatly excited by the thought of extra female competition to contend with. Indeed, I icily reply, her treachery is intolerable and I think that perhaps it's best we not see each other any more.

Sophie gulps, nods manfully, then watches with teary eyes as I lurch with great dignity out into the street and towards my car.

Tuesday   25 February
After suffering the indignity of spending half the night at police station being falsely accused of trying to break into someone else's Honda Civic which, in my slightly inebriated state, I mistakenly thought was mine (totally unaware that my own set of wheels had been clamped and towed away), hand over scandalous sum to car pound attendant and retire a beaten and broken woman to my new place in Kensington.

Wednesday   26 February
My hastily acquired rented abode is turning out to be full of unwelcome surprises, not least being the washing machine that I've just discovered lurking behind my bathroom door. The presence of this so-called 'modern convenience' means I can no longer justify myself to less progressive paramours when they ask me why I'm still using home-delivery laundry services.

Get another nasty shock when, on the way to collect and read the previous tenant's mail, I almost fall into, and over, the communal pool and gym respectively – both of which I hadn't previously cared to notice and both of which I have absolutely no intention of using so long as I'm naturally svelte.

I suspect, however, that as soon as the genetically plump fitness fanatics posing as my friends hear of these free and easy-to-access facilities, they'll be dropping by to see me with alarming regularity.

Thursday   27 February
Spend a fretful few hours shivering in my underwear, attempting

to start up the stupid twin tub so I have some clean clothes to wear. Add too much washing powder and end up doing a brilliant impression of a sud-wrestling female slipping and sliding across the bathroom floor. Eliza eventually comes to my rescue by showing up at the door under the pretext of being a caring, sharing friend whilst at the same time clutching a treacherous gym bag.

Leave her to heave and gasp in a most unattractive manner on an exercise bike, slip into her dress (which is a trifle loose since I'm at least two sizes smaller) and sneak off to Langan's because I'm meant to be meeting Frangipani and her new boyfriend.

Clearly terrified that her two-legged retirement fund might run off with me, Frangipani shows up alone. Judging by the expensive champagne she then insists upon pouring down my throat, I assume she's forgiven me for losing Leicester, her precious pug. This generosity of spirit on her part is nothing less than expected, however, since it's only due to my dog-ditching efforts that she's been able to cash in on his life assurance policies.

Friday   **28 February**

As predicted, word about my gym has got around. Ferguson and Phoebe both show up at my place with cheap house-warming presents for me in one hand and bathing caps and swimming goggles for them in the other.

After I've turned them away with instructions never to darken my door with toasters and cordial glasses under £20 again, Eliza calls to say her old Volkswagen broke down on the way back home last night and, thanks to me stealing her clothes, she had no choice but to greet the Royal Automobile (RAC) man clad only in a G-string leotard, thus scoring her first proper date in over three years.

I just love the way some of my friends turn my terrible misfortunes into their own remarkable good luck.

PART III

Saturday   **1 March**

This afternoon, whilst my face was being stripped with fruit acids and smothered in sheep's membranes, another Katya entered this world.

I wished I could have been there for her ungainly, rather amateurish debut but, like I said to a frantically puffing and panting Angel when I hauled her, her overnight bag and my camcorder out on to the pavement outside the hospital early this morning, I'd really prefer not to witness 12 hours of natural labour for I suspect it might be enough to put me off men for life – and I really don't need any more help in that department.

Besides, I didn't want to miss my facial and I figured I could always catch the birth on video later.

Of course, since I was the only friend brave enough to attempt to squeeze a 13-stone woman into a Honda Civic hatchback at the risk of her waters breaking over my pristine grey upholstery, I did make Angel promise she'd name her newborn child after me, regardless of its sex. (Was secretly hoping for a boy so yet another member of the male species could be the subject of constant ridicule, thanks to yours truly.)

Sunday   **2 March**

Armed with cigars, champers and a non-gender-specific toy monster I found in my cornflakes box at breakfast, head for public maternity ward to visit my godchild and namesake.

Its mother looks a complete wreck and makes me feel a mite guilty about intentionally appearing at my glamorous best. Angel hands me little Katya who, in promising protégée form, starts screaming blue murder. Promptly hand the bawling bundle back to Angel, declaring it looks just like her, though to be honest it's actually the spitting image of Bogie Boy – albeit with less hair and more conversation.

When I then sarcastically ask, through narrowed eyes and between puffs on my Cuban, where the other proud parent is, Angel bursts into a spasm of post-natal sobs and says he's gone on a three-day bender with all his brain-dead friends.

Monday   **3 March**

Go to supermarket to stock up on biros because I refuse to sign copies of my forthcoming tome using my expensive Mont Blanc refills. Oddly enough, not once do I harbour feelings of ill-will towards the tearaway toddlers that always seem to get themselves trapped between the wheels of my trolley. I must be feeling broody.

Of course, when I arrive at the check-out and proceed to get ticked off by a sullen teen for going through the express lane with 80 individual pens, biological clock stops again. A good thing, really, I later think to myself as I climb into my bed alone for the umpteenth night in a row, given that immaculate conception only ever seems to happen to virgins.

Tuesday   **4 March**

Today, after checking the condom vending machine that doubles as my purse, I realise that not one of the 48 items inside is missing – despite the fact I restocked well over two weeks ago.*

Eliza arrives bang in the middle of my romantic stocktake and very patronisingly offers to set me up with one of her RAC beau's work colleagues. I tactfully decline, saying thanks but I can afford to get my Honda Civic regularly serviced so, unlike *some* I could mention, I don't have to resort to dating a roadside emergency repair man in order to get it fixed on the cheap.

Also tersely remind Eliza of the Curse of Namambo, telling her it's wrong to be endangering someone's life so wilfully – even if he does wear overalls for a living. Unfortunately, it seems that Eliza has beaten me to it this time and has already told her new love about her dark and tragic secret. She reckons he reckons he's perfectly willing to take the risk of unforeseen accidents and has even taken out extra medical insurance to prove his intentions are true.

When she's gone off to collect him from casualty (he fell down an uncovered manhole yesterday evening), settle back down to the pile of prophylactics in front of me. Relying heavily upon short-term memory loss, plus a certain degree of self-deception

*See Friday, 14 February.

surreptitiously ditch 12 of the triple-rib specials, nine of the Donkey Deluxes and a Jolly Roger.

Immediately start feeling better again.

Wednesday   5 March

Whilst practising signing on cheques to greedy, grabbing bulk-pack condom mail-order companies with an illustrious and elaborate flourish, my publisher's publicist rings to say she may be able to secure me an interview with a leading women's magazine. Having already anticipated my first breathless question, publicist adds that no, they probably won't want me on the cover. Apparently, I would be considered too 'mature' and, instead, my celebrity profile is more than likely to be placed between the home-cooking hints and a feature on needlepoint.

As if this wasn't bad enough, receive one of those stupid chain-mail letters in the post. It says that if I don't do as it says, I'll end up sad, fat and on the shelf by the time I'm 40. Although confident such a fate will never befall me, feel duty-bound to spend the day photocopying and then faxing copies of said letter to ten of my more superstitious, single female friends.

Thursday   6 March

This morning, on my way back from procuring another well-deserved pay rise from my *London Goss* editor who realises the importance of keeping an about-to-be-too-famous-to-bother-writing-a-lowly-little-column author happy, sashay past a building site. Inwardly steeling myself for inevitable hoary hoots and lewd remarks from the blue-collared cavemen pretending to be hard at work six storeys above, my horror is indescribable when I don't receive so much as a single wolf whistle.

Thinking my guaranteed-grunt boys might not have spotted me (though I can't see how since I'm sure it's not every day they see a woman saunter ostentatiously past at such a leisurely, possibly even snail-like, pace – most females tending to scuttle by with head down and arms firmly strapped across bosom), I turn back around and retrace my footsteps. Not even a catcall.

Am thus forced to check and see if my previously appreciative audience hasn't fallen off the scaffolding. Clamber on to the platform only to find six red-blooded wildebeest lounging about and, worse still, looking directly my way with a distinct lack of interest.

In subsequent mad dash to crash-course in self-esteem building (the Atlantic Bar, 6 p.m.–10 p.m.), get stopped for speeding down Shaftesbury Avenue, which is hugely unjust since the police car must have been going at least 70 miles per hour in order to overtake me, cut me off and bring my Honda Civic hatchback to a screeching halt. Nonetheless, brace myself for the *de rigueur* mock-stern lecture, the usual light and lingering rap on the knuckles, and the torn-up ticket. Am instead presented with a whopping great fine by an acne-faced adolescent who seems totally immune to my girlish charms.

Naturally, am not feeling too young and carefree when I totter into the Atlantic Bar. But, doing my perky best, ask an elderly patron how old he thinks I am. He seems inordinately pleased with himself when he gets it right first guess. Needless to say, I don't finish the drink he's bought me, well, I can't now he's wearing all of it.

Friday   **7 March**
Tut-tut with disapproval when I learn through this morning's newspaper that students are protesting again about university fees. In my day, I would have just asked my parents for it. Anyway, I don't know what the ungrateful brats have got to complain about since, unlike some of us, at least they've got their *youth*.

Try and turn back the hands of time in evening by meeting up with mistress Phoebe. In her presence, I always feel I look at least ten years younger, mostly because I am. Sardonically suggest we head for the cramped dining quarters of the French House in Soho in the hope I might be able to rub my wizened shoulders with men who like a fine vintage woman. My mortification knows no limits when a waiter, clearly thinking I've left my walking frame at home, gently takes my elbow and guides me to our table.

When he then stumbles off, with a nose that wasn't bleeding

and broken just moments before, Phoebe cautiously suggests I'm being over-sensitive. This, I think, is a bit rich coming from she who once decked a bus conductor for making a couple of pregnant mothers forfeit their seats for her.

Saturday   8 March
Late this morning Eliza calls. It seems she's obsessed with reversing my single, celibate status – despite my vehement protests about how I like being lonely and bitter. Indeed, she's taken it upon herself to set me up on a blind date tonight with someone I haven't even *met* before . . . However, she does warn me that he's as wary of the whole desperate arrangement as I am, is only in it for a light-hearted fling and will probably beg off at the last minute anyway.

Mid afternoon, decide to beat my blind date to it by reneging on him first. Call Eliza and cancel tonight's dinner plans. Tell her that now that I'm getting on a bit, I'm not into light-hearted flings any more.

In early evening, Eliza rings back to say Mr Anonymous's appetite has been seriously whetted by my unintentional lack of availability. He's now so keen to meet me, he's willing to start talking commitment sight unseen.

At this rate, I should be able to wrangle a marriage proposal before our first date.

Sunday   9 March
Today, I have to go and watch world premiere screening of *Katya the Second* at Angel's place in Tottenham. Slightly jealous of all the attention my baby peer is getting after only eight measly days on this earth, but try and be adult about it by consoling myself that it'll be at least another 16 years before she's any real threat.

As it turns out, I inadvertently steal the show anyway when I faint during the uncut Caesarean scene.

Monday   10 March
Have decided am not going to age gracefully after all. Ring the only

male I know who likes me for my personality and not my rapidly fading looks, and ask for a referral to a top-notch cosmetic surgeon.

Unfortunately, I don't quite catch the good doctor's name because Ferguson's just had his lips pumped full of Goretex. Until the swelling goes down and he starts making sense again, am just going to have to follow in the doddery tracks of faded film stars and make do with a piece of fishing line and a couple of clothes pegs.

This puts me in a bit of a bind as I'm meant to be once again meeting my blind date tonight. According to Eliza, Mr Anonymous has organised a 'surprise' hot-air balloon ride to a field in Surrey with dinner to follow. Since I look a sight for sore eyes and since he appears so keen and I'd like to keep it that way, use the oldest man-baiting trick in the book. Ring him an hour before take-off and cancel.

Tuesday   **11 March**
Thanks to selfish, thoughtless and completely bone-idle public transport workers who'll use any old excuse to shirk work and go on strike, my Macedonian cleaner turns up many hours late for work today. She's had to travel all the way from Arsenal to my place on foot, which can't be good for her arthritis.

Help make her more comfortable by guiding her down on to her hands and knees so she can scrub my kitchen floor. Then stand over her to ensure she doesn't sweep debris under the fridge as she is wont to do when my back is turned.

Whilst attempting to pick up crumbs with gnarled and twisted fingers, because I haven't got round to buying a broom yet, she cheerfully informs me that she's been taking art classes in order to 'better herself'. She goes on to add that she's planning to enter the Royal Academy of Arts Portrait Competition and, furthermore, is looking for a British notable to sit for her.

I, of course, say I'll only pose if I can have half her winnings *and* get a further discount on all her future domestic duties. She appears touched by my *noblesse oblige* but eventually demurs –

though not before flattering me immensely by saying she's looking for someone more venerable (i.e. *older*).

Remove clothes pegs and fishing line.

Wednesday   12 March

In preparation for book publicity onslaught next week, decide to set up my very own personal Web site so adoring male fans can post me their words of worship and credit card details.

Thursday   13 March

3½ Minutes (Can Seem Like A Lifetime) arrives in all quality bookshops and bargain stores today. Because my publisher is too mean to put on a lavish launch, make Teddington swallow his envy and accompany me on an ad hoc promotional tour of my own.

Spend hours racing round my neighbourhood removing copies of my literary tome from obscure corners and then liberally scattering them round prime-position shelves. Manager at Books Etc seems somewhat shocked when I plonk myself at the counter with biros at the ready and then proceed to make customers line up for signed copies. Everyone is clearly humbled, though, especially the motorcycle courier who only came in to drop off a package – except for the sales assistant who decides to use his precious first edition as a coffee-cup coaster.

Friday   14 March

Check my personal Web site for on-line admirers. Only one today is 'Hank' who assures me he's a stockbroker in Manhattan, though, judging by his appalling grammar, he must have got into Harvard on scholarship. Typically, right at the climactic moment, and just when Hank is about to reveal his net worth, my laptop has a power surge, leaving me in a state of *cyber interruptus*.

Romantic endeavours thus thwarted, head off to Eliza's place in Camden because I've decided to accompany her and RAC Man to a Fear and Loathing party down in Kent. Eliza seems somewhat surprised to see me since I'd agreed to meet with Mr Anonymous down by the Thames tonight. However, like I loftily tell her as I throw my Louis Vuitton luggage into the back of her swain's breakdown van, being left to cruise/dine by himself should only serve to make him crave me more.

On our subsequent trip south, notice RAC Man is already showing signs of the scourge of Namambo. Fortunately for Eliza, he doesn't appear too perturbed. I, on the other hand, find it enormously disconcerting to be driven round hairpin bends by a man with a patch on one eye, an arm in a sling and both legs in splints. Indeed, it would be quite fair to say I'm a total and utter gibbering wreck in the back seat.

Three bottles of champers and half a medicine cabinet later, fall out the back of the van and float into cottage relatively unscathed.

Saturday   15 March
Wake up with rotten hangover. RAC Man makes pathetic attempt to open beer bottles with his teeth to accompany completely inedible breakfast that Eliza's dished up for her motley crew of friends.

Afterwards, RAC Man and the rest of the menfolk go hunting and gathering at the local snooker hall whilst us women stay back and do dishes. Pick up a tea towel and wave it about in a busy manner. Then go and sit in a comfy corner and read *3½ Minutes* in the foolish hope someone will ask me who it was written by.

In the evening, an elaborate pre-party feast is prepared, but I make my stand for feminism again by following the men's example and do nothing whatsoever to contribute.

Ugly scene transpires later on when five knuckle-headed types gatecrash and proceed to fight for my favours. Sadly, none of them are my type, so leave them blind-siding each other with their six-packs of lager and retire to my bed, only to discover a stray hopeful has seconded my bunk.

Kick him out, then check the sheets for fleas.

Sunday   16 March
Wake up hideously hung over again. Everyone wants to bond with nature and take a nice freezing-cold walk (or crawl, in the case of

Eliza's beau) in the countryside. I beg off by saying I've just got to finish the book I'm currently reading because it's written by a very talented author.

One of RAC Man's simian cohorts said he read it earlier and thought it was full of crap. Retort rapier-like that he try reading it the correct way up next time.

Get home early evening. Check book for crap bits.

Monday   **17 March**

Receive further savaging from 'literary' critics. *'A shocking piece of filth. . .'* gasps one. *'Not worth the paper it's printed on. . .'* sniffs another.

Write stroppy letter back to them both saying that I would have expected them to be a little more supportive of their own flesh-and-blood's achievements.

Tuesday   **18 March**

Have to get up extra-early for on-air interview with London radio station. Resulting foul mood not soothed when idiot DJ asks me what my book is about.

Try reading it, I snarl before abruptly hanging up.

Late afternoon, publisher's hard-nosed publicist rings to admonish me for snubbing Mr DJ and even threatens to cancel my telly interview tomorrow. Retaliate by saying my phone got cut off mid-air because, as an author of a particularly mean publisher, I'm too poor to pay my phone bill. Besides, since I'm rarely out of bed before noon, I'd specifically requested *not* to be interviewed on a breakfast show – particular one on *community* radio.

Wednesday   **19 March**

Have to go to TV station to promote *3½ Minutes (Can Seem Like A Lifetime)* on afternoon talk show. Cab driver takes me the long route, no doubt trying to pluck up the courage to ask me for my autograph (which I wasn't going to give to him anyway).

Once at TV station, a make-up artist asks me if I'm allergic to any particular type of eyeshadow. Pink and purple, I pointedly reply. Must say, she did a surprisingly good job considering she had the cosmetic equivalent of tarting up a Monet.

Hustled on to set by a harried-looking producer who warns me that the show is in a state of chaos and confusion because some old war veteran has locked his keys in his car, thereby throwing the timing schedule out of whack.

This excuse makes about as much sense as the subsequent interview I have with a couch-ridden talking head who thinks I'm here to talk about laxatives – tempted to put him straight but, not wishing to embarrass him in his twilight years, humour him and wax lyrically about the weight-loss benefits of Ex Lax.

Thursday   20 March
In rush-hour traffic today in Kensington, some housewife pulls out in front of my Honda Civic hatchback, beeps her horn, winds down her window and starts screaming hysterically, saying how she saw me on telly yesterday. Cringe behind my steering wheel, fervently wishing I could do what other celebrities do and take to her bonnet with a golf club.

Since the pressures of fame are clearly getting to me, pop into nearest High Street pub for a calming quaff. No sooner do I do that, catch some TV cameramen clustered behind the doorway. Cover my face with my Prada bag and mutter 'no comment', only to be advised by bald-faced lying bar staff that the crew is here to shoot a fly-on-the-wall documentary not to follow a fabulously famous author around.

Friday   21 March
In anticipation of more harassment from media and general public alike, have barricaded myself inside my apartment, sandbagged my letter box and taken the phone off the hook.

Saturday   22 March
Relieved to report not so much as a single knock on the door for the past 48 hours.

Sunday   **23 March**

Check my flat's foyer thoroughly for random members of the paparazzi and find myself besieged only by filthy-rich Frangipani who's 'just popped by' to triumphantly brandish a diamond the size of my laptop in front of my face. Having cunningly and connivingly kept me out of her merchant banker's lustful reach, it seems she's at last managed to secure a marriage proposal from him.

Take to bed feeling extremely ill.

Monday   **24 March**

Put phone back on hook and then curse myself bitterly because the only caller is Teddington ringing to say he's just found out he's an adopted child. This, of course, comes as no surprise to me. Like I remind him in as kind a manner as humanly possible, I've always thought it odd how his folks are highly respected professionals in their fields whilst Teddington hasn't got a talented bone in his body.

Think I managed to convince him not to track his real parents down by warning him about the potential ignominy of discovering they both work for the civil service.

Tuesday   **25 March**

Ferguson is also now not speaking to me.

Thoroughly bored of being holed up at home waiting for press siege, and knowing full well that he was just about to don a tuxedo, throw a box of instant popcorn in the microwave and get all a-quiver in anticipation of watching the Oscars tonight, decided to amuse myself by rattling off the winners in quick succession down the phone at him after watching the late-afternoon news bulletin. I do this to him every year so you'd think he'd have learnt to see the funny side by now.

Wednesday   **26 March**

Obviously keen to brush-up on foreign foreplay techniques, Mistress Phoebe drops by and drags me from my self-imposed exile and into some arthouse cinema whereupon she expects me to shell out my hard-earned cash for the sort of film I can see on Channel Four for free.

When I walk out of the place halfway through it, a bunch of Japanese photographers aim their lenses my way and gesture madly. Just as I'm about to give them a piece of my mind for press intrusion, they have the gall to say they want *me* to take photographs of *them.*

Thursday   **27 March**
Getting slightly miffed at my treatment (or lack thereof) at the hands of the media – which is probably why I am in no mood to sympathise with my agent's current woes.

Indeed, sit and get appallingly drunk at the bar at the Savoy because it's slightly more interesting than listening to her bang on about how I am her least profitable client ever. Indeed, she drones on in injured tones, my publisher's accountants are considering charging her for the leviathan lawyer's bill they've racked up on my behalf.

Apparently, every other word in *3½ Minutes* is libellous, slanderous or defamatory and, more often than not, all three. What's more, finally sick of being the butt of all jokes about men who are faster than a flu jab, Mr Dud is threatening to sue. (Though how he's going to prove in a public court of law that he can last longer than an egg-timer is completely beyond me.)

Friday   **28 March**
                                                               Good Friday
Have just been stood up for hot cross buns at Maison Bertaux by Mr Anonymous. It seems my recent coquettish plans have badly backfired and my constant cancellations have sent him heading for the hills.

Extreme melancholia not much helped when I then have to go and do lunch with Angel and young Katya at Café Bohème. Whilst Katya Junior regurgitates mother's milk all over my plate of rocket, the waiter stands by and coos inanities, completely oblivious to the more attractive Katya Senior dry-retching into her tote.

Morbid depression continues unabated through evening, even though I then get to dine at Langan's with Frangipani and her new merchant banker fiancé. She foolishly thinking it's safe for me to meet him now he's signed the pre-nups. However, just in case he is tempted to cast caution, and half his gold shares, to the wind, she's taken some precautionary measures and invited some of his childless and chinless colleagues along to distract me.

Since I would never dream of personally rendering any of them daddies, I sit and get rat-arsed at their expense and amuse the table (and the ones nearby) with raucous impressions of Angel's antics at lunchtime.

By the end of the night, Frangipani seems strangely subdued. Indeed, she departs just before I've finished my meal and well before she's handed over her AmEx to pay for it. Suspect my jealous pal can't cope with the fact my décolletage is attracting so much attention from her new fiancé.

Saturday   **29 March**

Have to screen all my calls today because I'm terrified Angel is going to ask me to make good my offer to baby-sit my godchild like I'd promised her yesterday before I said yes this morning to Ferguson's rather more enticing invitation to go fag-hagging down Old Compton Street.

However, the only message on my machine is from the latter who allegedly claims he's at a local burns unit getting emergency skin grafts. He goes on to say that he fell asleep at the solarium this afternoon and now has third-degree burns to nine-tenths of his body. Judging from the telltale background noises, unless the Royal Free Hospital has started piping trance music through its tannoy, I suspect Ferguson may have had a better offer.

This is just typical of the sort of selfish, opportunistic people I tend to attract.

Sunday   **30 March**
                                                          Easter Sunday

Whilst whipping up a batch of festive eggnogs, phone rings.

Without thinking, pick it up. Dismayed to hear Angel asking me if I can look after young Katya tonight because Bogie Boy wants to attempt a reconciliation – no doubt in the back of his van in a Hammersmith carpark where the whole sorry affair began.

Much as I am a champion of happy couples, and not in the least bit bitter about my own solitary state, I have to refuse because I don't want to catch whooping cough. Promise Angel I'll make myself available as soon as the baby gets her vaccinations and makes it past puberty.

Then head off for a girls-only night at Eliza's place because her RAC beau is currently getting his face stitched back together after walking into a lamppost this morning.

Having received an unfairly large redundancy package from my former place of employ which is still rationalising at an alarming rate, Eliza informs me she's thinking of investing in an up-market vegan restaurant in Islington. Judging by the fare she's just dished up, I'm tempted to say she'd be better off opening a food stall in Brixton. However, wisely keep my mouth shut because I was taught never to open it when chewing on relentlessly tough bits of nut cutlet.

Monday   31 March
Easter Monday

Call all emergency services, plus members of the media, after waking up at four in the morning with suspected case of botulism from the last supper I shall ever eat at Eliza's Diner. On way to hospital, flirt feebly with ambulance officer and, upon arrival, smile wanly but winsomely for benefit of paparazzi.

Extremely embarrassed when extensive tests show I merely have a mild dose of the flu which I think I must have caught off the Young Liberal Democrat I met the other night* – though I can't be sure for certain since events turned slightly hazy after the fifteenth vodka he bought me in a futile attempt to earn my respect.

Exit ward to thunderous looks from the press corps and pitying stares from medical staff and hail nearby cab clutching a box of

See Friday, 28 March.

Lemsip plus the phone numbers of two firemen, an orderly and aforementioned ambulance officer.

Get home to hear my agent on my answering machine pleading with me to call. Only do so because I presume it must be urgent since she barely toils enough on my behalf during working hours, let alone on public holidays.

Tuesday   1 April
April Fool's Day

England's foremost diarist, Katya Livingston, would like to apologise to readers – male or otherwise – for the absence of her column in today's issue of London Goss. *She is suffering from a particularly vicious bout of morning sickness. She should be back on board next week.*

Wednesday   2 April

Through no real fault of my own, I have managed to weave a tangled web of truly ridiculous proportions. This is because yesterday I told my *London Goss* editor I was suffering from 'morning sickness', foolishly thinking that he, like most members of the press, would be all too *au fait* with this euphemism for drinking 28 vodka martinis in a row the night before a newspaper deadline in an attempt to forget the humiliation of having my book pulped due to lack of sales, threat of legal action and the fact that I made the entire story up in what I hoped would prove to be the biggest cultural hoax in British history.

What I had not realised was that my editor is part of the new and scary wave of teetotal journalism, so he took my words literally and proceeded to devote three column centimetres to my mythical motherhood. Consequently, I'm being besieged by knitted bootees, support tights and haemorrhoid creams from misguided *London Goss* fans, not to mention some extremely frantic calls from right-to-life types who seem ready to renege on their previous hard-line policies.

To make matters worse, my silver-tongued solicitor has just rung to inform me that my unborn child is already being sued for custody by no less than 32 male hopefuls, only 30 of whom I remember sleeping with.

Thursday   3 April

Am starting to quite like all this attention as a purported mother-to-be. Even the usually belligerent *London Goss* sub-editors have started nagging me about the whereabouts of my column in softer, more soothing tones. Since there is every possibility that I might at last get the extensive press coverage I deserve, I may well see out the full term of my phantom pregnancy.

Friday   4 April

Receive set-of-three romper suits from my mother, express post. Promptly add them to the ever-mounting pile of useless baby paraphernalia that is cluttering my walk-in wardrobe. Even if, on the remotest off-chance I do ever manage to conceive, no child of mine will be seen crawling up and down King's Road in terry towelling.

Saturday   5 April

Well aware my flat's entrance could be blockaded by cameras and microphones but nonetheless determined to gatecrash engagement party at Frangipani's pile in Primrose Hill, enlist the help of Ferguson who, having not got a date for tonight, has nothing better to do than don a maternity smock and affect a particularly unprepossessing impression of me sashaying out the front door to greet maternal-minded media.

I, in turn, clad in a more suitable diaphanous dress by Ghost and fetching non-support La Perla bra, sneak out the back way, slip into my car and drive recklessly through what I hope and pray are media hordes, taking great relish in watching them bounce off the paint work.

Engagement party is in full swing by the time I get there. Indeed there are at least 20 people hovering listlessly about in the ballroom. One of them, a highly respected columnist for a national broadsheet approaches me and proffers his hand, saying his nine-year-old granddaughter is a great admirer of my *London Goss* column. Am thus forced to repay the compliment and assure him that my 87-year-old great-grandmother is an admirer of his work. Bathed as we are in afterglow of mutual admiration, his wallflower wife glowers at me and stabs a skewer into a passing meatball in a particularly foreboding way.

Frangipani doesn't seem too pleased to see me but puts on a brave face in front of her fiancé who seems inordinately interested in the cut and line of my fabulous frock.

Proceed to spend early hours of morning fending off drunken lechers who re-enact their midlife crisis on the dance floor and think it is their right to maul me just because I am dressed in a non-hermetically sealed dress.

Manage to get home before sunrise – which I am then forced to sit and watch from the discomfort of the front entrance of my apartment block because I am too inebriated to drag myself up the three steps to my front door.

Sunday   6 April
Wake up in rose bushes feeling nauseous, thanks to the bowl of punch I drank last night and which I think might have been spiked with tinned fruit.

Don't feel much better when, upon perusing the late edition of today's paper, I fail to see a photo of me at Frangipani's engagement party being the reluctant recipient of male pawing en masse while headline screams: MUM-TO-BE SEEN ENJOYING HERSELF!!!

Monday   7 April
Extremely unfit mother Angel arrives at my door wheezing and gasping under the weight of Katya Junior and the litre bottle of vodka I requested she cunningly hide in the carrycot away from prying paparazzi pregnancy police.

She tries to convince me to ditch my elaborate charade, saying I will have to gain a lot more weight over the next few months if I wish to effect a convincing duck-like gait.

Since I refuse to eat for one, let alone two, she may very well have a point.

Tuesday   8 April

Having just received a first and final warning from my *London Goss* editor for admitting I faked my own pregnancy, plus an unnecessarily terse rejection letter from my publisher about my suggested follow-up to *3½ Minutes* (working title: *9½ Months and Regretting It Dearly*), I fear my star is on the wane.

Against my better judgement, ring my useless agent for some wise advice. She says, only half-jokingly, that I should do what other ambitious desperadoes do and get a role on *Brookside.* Hang up on her at once, furious she dare even suggest I sacrifice my artistic integrity by selling my soul to commercial TV.

Wednesday   9 April

Have decided to take infinitely more respectable shortcut to fame and fortune and sell my body to an upmarket men's magazine.

Kindly receptionist at *The Economist* tells me they don't do centrefolds, so I am forced to lower my high moral standards somewhat and ring up the airbrush artist of a more risqué rag who in turn tells me that soap stars are usually more saleable commodities than literary authors, but to send in my vitals anyway.

Post off a couple of polaroids that my Macedonian cleaner has yet to steal and then flog to the media – mainly because she's too lazy to vacuum under my bed.

Thursday   10 April

In preparation for my defrocking debut, have decided to embark upon a short-term bout of celibacy – mainly because I don't want some faceless stranger going to the press with, MY NIGHT OF WANTON ABANDON WITH CENTREFOLD!!! Thus damaging my carefully cultivated image as a high-minded, bookish kind of bunny.

Make good my intentions by heading off to B&Q store to purchase some spigots and rivets for my do-it-yourself chastity belt. You can imagine my complete lack of surprise when I spy

Sebastian the Beelzebub serving behind the spare-parts counter. Having been sacked from McDonald's after a mystery customer complained she saw him fondling the merchandise, he shows me to the appropriate section.

Indeed, he seems suspiciously eager to assist me in my quest for semi-permanent purity.

Friday   11 April
Turn down all offers to troll London's dens of iniquity as I can no longer wear figure-hugging fanbelts now that I am encased in a steel-plated man-repeller. Conduct my social life down the phone instead.

First bit of excitement is from Ferguson who rings me up in a flood of girlish tears. Following a doomed affair with the owner of a chain of shopping-centre hairdressing salons, he's been left with nought but a tragic perm and a desire to go into hiding until it grows out. I, of course, tell him it's his own stupid fault for being dumb enough to date someone called 'Gino' in the first place.

No sooner does Ferguson slam down the phone, Calliope calls to say she's in California and has stacked on ten kilos trying to eat her way out of the subsequent deep and dark depression. Am extremely disturbed to hear this news because Calliope was never particularly fine-boned to start off with.

Am not too happy about her choice of destination, either. She's actually meant to be setting up house in Jersey so I've got somewhere to stay next year on my way to a tax-avoidance scheme cleverly disguised as my regional Playmate of the Year tour.

Saturday   12 April
In awe of my immense good taste, Angel begs me to go to a furniture auction with her in Hackney because she's unable to afford to buy a second-hand pram from a more salubrious suburb now that she's a single mother. Only agree to go because the types I'll meet out there are hardly likely to lead me into sexual temptation.

Receive an odd look from Angel when she comes to pick me up, kaftans not being my usual mode of attire. Indeed, she politely inquires as to why I'm wearing one. Cast her a baleful glare and tell her that my Dawn French special is of little social significance to one who dresses courtesy of C&A's discount bin.

Since Angel still looks at me blankly, I then go on to patiently and slowly explain that I'm. Dressed. In. Designer. Shrouds. Because. I'm. Trying. To. Keep. Men. At. A. Distance. Angel raises an ill-plucked eyebrow and says that she didn't realise I had to go to such drastic measures in order to achieve this.

At auction, some idiot tries to outbid my friend so I stick my hand up on her behalf. Must say, she doesn't seem particularly thrilled that I've just landed her with a broken-down perambulator for a pound more than she wanted to spend.

Sunday   13 April

Since I am now unable to sneeze, breathe, chase after men or do anything else remotely functional, drive over to Ferguson's place in Hampstead just in time to witness him preparing to swallow an entire bottle of hair dye in an attempt to forget about Gino and his bad perming techniques.

Drag my melodramatic pal by the unbleached roots of his hair to the kitchen, snip off his Afro using a bread knife, march into the courtyard, hold a small but nonetheless touching service and, as a mark of disrespect for the man who has managed to make Ferguson look worse than I ever thought possible, throw the offending frizz into a shallow grave and set it alight.

In a fit of pansy passion, Ferguson then throws himself on to the pyre, thereby singeing his remaining locks and compelling me to unceremoniously douse him with the contents from the bottle of 'Blonde' by Versace that I happen to have handy.

Needless to say, old Cinders bids me a rather speedy farewell before racing off to Toni & Guy Hair Salon to rescue what's left of his piebald pate.

Monday   14 April

Receive letter from editor of men's magazine thanking me kindly for the polaroids and the unpadded 36C bra I sent him. He says that whilst my physical endowments more than suffice, my intelligence quotient is far too high and, indeed, may frighten off some of his readers. (Suspect that listing my ideal man as 'dead' and my favourite hobby as 'splitting atoms' did nothing to help my cause. The fact I was actually capable of filling in the 'Bunny Profile' without the aid of some hack male staffer probably went against me too.)

Cheered by the thought that at least now I can take off my chastity belt.

Tuesday   15 April
Still trying to unlock stupid belt. Sebastian, that Satan's Apprentice Hardware Assistant From Hell, must have deliberately given me the wrong-sized key.

Terrified I'll be forced to live like a nun for the rest of my life – as opposed to the five days thus far – call Eliza's boyfriend for help because the RAC are supposed to be good in emergencies. He obligingly limps round within the hour, jump leads and spanners in tow. After an utterly futile one-armed wrestle with my industrial-strength knickers, he sadly informs me that it's going to take a blowtorch to get them off.

Wednesday   16 April
Following an extremely tortuous and potentially scandalous tug-of-war with the London Fire Brigade, am now free from the vice-like grip of the solid steel panty girdle I so impulsively strapped to my person. Of course, the private shame of being set upon with the jaws-of-life and a tub of Vaseline by three strapping young men who then refused to do a couple of other little odd jobs around my flat for me was nothing compared to the public embarrassment of having to admit that I don't know how to change the light bulbs in my living-room overheads.

Since I refuse point-blank to watch *The X-Files* in the dark because it's a well-known fact that squinting causes crows feet, drive over to Angel's place in Tottenham to watch it there. She immediately leaves me to play surrogate mum to her yapping baby whilst she swans off to bingo with Bogie Boy. Not wanting a repeat performance of Katya's usual high and extremely noisy theatrics, because Mulder rarely moves his lips even when he's speaking, add a splash of Gordon's gin to my young charge's formula. Needless to say, she sleeps unlike a baby.

When her mother gets home at one in the morning with Bogie Boy in tow, little Katya positively screams the house down so I assume at least one person doesn't want me to go. On the contrary, her mother grimly informs me, waggling the empty Gordon's bottle in my face. Thanks to my bad influence, my godchild is suffering her very first hangover.

Thursday   17 April
Am horrified to learn today that the inner suburbs are about to be invaded by plagues of rats because this means if I'm determined to prove I can do anything without the aid of a man, am going to have to scurry down to local supermarket to buy cheese slices and other household poisons.

Several hours of panic buying and lethal interior landscaping later, am confident that no furry-faced creature will ever get to sink its fangs into me unless, that is, it comes equipped with two opposable thumbs and a desire to commit.

In the evening, have to leave my ill-lit lair and head for Freedom for Ferguson's send-off.

After a series of disastrous relationships and beautification programmes, Ferguson has now quit his job at the escort agency and decided to go find himself in India – though personally I think he'd be better off finding a shrink in London. But no. There he sits, cross-legged on top of the bar, frocked up in a sari and baring a freshly waxed chest and scalp. Deeply embarrassed on his behalf, toss him a gift-wrapped box of all-purpose dysentery and diphtheria tablets from a safe distance, then leave before anyone important recognises me.

Friday   18 April
Spend most of the day hopping about on one foot because the

other has a fiendishly tenacious rat trap attached to it. Thanks to current lack of artificial lighting, I stumbled blindly into my abode last night, completely forgetting I had turned it into a den of death just a few hours before. Only when my palely polished toenails begin to look like they've been doused in Chanel Vamp do I once again reluctantly enlist the help of a more mechanically minded male.

Pest exterminator seems rather amused by my helpless plight, though his annoyingly loud guffaws soon turn to satisfyingly quiet little gagging noises after I slip some rat poison into his complimentary cup of tea.

Once he's departed – weaving slightly from his liberally laced tea – light up a couple of candles in readiment for nightfall.

Ambience spoilt somewhat when I spot a furry four-legged thing skitter alongside my living room skirting board. Brain it with a Vikram Seth epic and then haul it by its tail into my fridge-freezer.

Saturday   19 April

Finally run out of candles, so dial London Electricity's emergency faults service. Five hours later, an electrician arrives on my doorstep and appears slightly aggrieved to be called out just to install three bayonet globes.

Needless to say, he's quick to follow instructions when I open my frost-free fridge-freezer – though not before knowledgeably informing me that the perfectly iced rat grinning fixedly within is actually a squirrel and it's illegal to kill them.

Sunday   20 April

Head off to Saint Something's in Tottenham because Katya Junior is about to be baptised.

Am very cross when, after much tedious theologising – made bearable only by a sliver of Sunbeam Bread and a squirt of Cabernet Sauvignon – the priest dunks my bawling godchild far too devoutly into the font and leaves water stains on my brand new suede shirt.

Perhaps as a sign of her appreciation for me being the only member of the congregation who's bothered to turn up in dry-clean-only attire, my godchild's mother Angel then presents me with one of those simulated pets conceived in Japan by crackpots who copulate with computers for a living. Apparently, I am meant to feed the thing, play with it and pick it up when it cries. If I don't, says Angel, my virtual baby will die just to spite me.

Not wishing to be charged with the wilful neglect of a minor as well as the murder of a squirrel, I surreptitiously deposit my tiny foundling upon the steps of the church whilst it's still squawking for a nappy change.

Monday   21 April
Upon opening my frost-free and finding squirrel still wedged between a packet of Bird's Eye peas and a bottle of Absolut, decide to do what most women do to get away from their problems and do a spot of shopping. Furthermore, decide to do it in Honkers because I know just the person who'll finance my trip in order to get me out of the way until she's managed to yank her merchant banker fiancé down the aisle.

Tuesday   22 April
Slap Frangipani's AmEx down on counter at Heathrow, only to be informed that all flights to Hong Kong are full. Am surprised to hear this as I presumed people would be begging to flee from the onslaught of communism rather than pay to actually greet the thing. As a last resort, brandish my press badge about in an imperious manner – taking care to keep my thumb over the expiry date – and soon get assigned to a seat at the back of the plane near the toilets.

During the long haul over, spend many enjoyable hours lecturing flaky-faced stewardesses about the benefits of using a good moisturiser. Then, after touch-down, make a bee-line for the Peninsula Hotel because I've heard there are gold Rolls Royces parked out the front.

Condescending concierge asks if 'modom has a booking'. Not wishing to lose face or gain expensive hotel bills, think quickly on my feet, point to the turban-topped dignitary from Brunei lurking lecherously in lobby and say that I'm here to have tea with His Highness. My opportunistic little Lothario immediately whisks me off to his sumptuous suite, plies me with champagne and tiger balm, and then chases me round the king-sized bed waving a fistful of credit cards.

Make my stand for western beauties everywhere and hurl one-thousand-year-old, culturally significant porcelain in his path. Then lock myself in football-field-sized bathroom, yelling – albeit in slightly halting Malay – that I don't care how many billions of trillions he's got, I don't consort with dwarfs.

Wednesday   23 April

After a singularly uncomfortable night's sleep in pond-sized bathtub, slip out of suite Suzie Wong-like whilst my royal bene-factor lies snoring, blissfully unaware that his snakeskin wallet is slithering along out the door with me. Am utterly disgusted to learn that shops here open even later than the ones down King's Road. Forced to brave a good few hours in a noodle shop sipping weak green tea all the while wondering how, even after 156 years of British rule, the locals still haven't learnt how to make a decent brew.

Then, after spending the gross national product of an oil-rich tax-free country in Borneo, hop on to the wrong ferry back to Kowloon and end up on some backwater archipelago beset by mud cottages and chockful of pyjama-clad pensioners shuffling along with fishing rods.

To make matters worse I am then serenaded by the wailing strains of an open-air Beijing opera. Several horrifying hours later, ears bleeding profusely, another ferry arrives and I manage to make my way back to the mainland.

Despite the fact that I refuse to tip him, a very helpful street urchin directs me to the nearest B&B.

Thursday   24 April

Following a rat-infested, roach-ridden evening at Chungking

Mansions, beating off thieving German backpackers with my Prada bag (not to mention the indignity of being body-searched at midnight by Hong Kong police on the lookout for foreign pickpockets posing as prostitutes), decide to punish the prince's plastic again. Thanks to all local taxis being commandeered by Chinese tourists, I'm forced to take the Mass Transit Railway thereby missing my shopping stop completely.

With not an Issey Miyake boutique in sight, proceed to do battle with natives who make the annual clearance sale at Harrods look like a bowls convention. Of course, after wafting passed the umpteenth tofu stall, start feeling intensely nauseous so stagger into the nearest pharmacy which turns out to be run by some dodgy herbalist who I'm sure then prescribes me with ground giant panda balls.

Come nightfall, still lost, and still picking medicinal bits from my teeth.

Friday   **25 April**

After spending absolutely hideous night lying upon a rattan mat with only a wooden block for a pillow and some exceptionally untalkative types as bed mates – all of whom kept me awake with their constant sucking on long-stemmed pipes – throw myself in the path of oncoming taxi and insist driver take me to airport. Skulk around airport duty-free shops for about five hours until my plane arrives.

When it does, am still too traumatised to even bother noticing the Chinese businessman beside me casting covetous looks my way. Only realise when he opens his wallet, produces a wad of travellers cheques and asks if I'd consider his hand in marriage. Whilst I am used to men impetuously proposing to me, am somewhat distrustful of his motives because usually they offer me a lot more than ten thousand pounds. Thus have to rudely rebuff his overtures, telling him I refuse to wed a man who can't roll his r's properly.

Get home. Unpack duty-free bags. Too tired to sleep so go to fridge-freezer to retrieve bottle of Absolut. Squirrel still there, suspended in Pleistocene animation.

Saturday   **26 April**

Thanks to the giant rat stashed in the depths of my fridge-freezer, my electricity expenses have gone through the roof this month. Judging by the bill I am currently holding between ice-blue fingertips, the people at London Electricity have decided to charge me handsomely for running my overworked white-goods appliance – despite the fact it's meant to have a five-star energy rating.

If this wasn't bad enough, London's typical spring weather is serving as a chill reminder of my snap-frozen fauna's unwelcome presence since it's absolutely freezing. Indeed, I'm having to write this *London Goss* column with no less than four recently acquired mini blow-heaters* at my feet.

Whilst attaching another three heaters to my multi-adaptor circuit board, two members from some nosy conservation group bang on my door to tell me they're following up a lead from the London Electricity technician. Like most self-respecting animal killers about to be falsely accused of murdering rare, endangered wildlife, I lie through my teeth and deny all charges, including the one about causing fire hazards in a densely populated apartment block. They both appear uncommonly interested in my recently registered cryogenics corporation so toss them an ice pick and leave them to it because I have more important things to do – like go to Eliza's place and beg for an alibi.

Unfortunately, Eliza's a little distracted too. Not only has RAC Man just been whisked off to hospital for a brain scan after a piece of disused Russian satellite fell on his head, but she's also lost her precious Persian cat. Indeed, she seems surprisingly unmoved by my possible life sentence for mistakenly slaughtering a squirrel. Instead, she rabbits on about how, after enlisting the help of a psychic to locate her feline hairball, she's planning to spend the next few hours searching for 'a pillared, pilloried pile where mad hounds bay at the moon'.

Leave her to it because, quite frankly, crawling round the Houses of Parliament and yelling 'Fluffy!' at the top of my lungs is not my idea of a fun night out.

See Friday, 23 April.

Sunday   **27 April**

Wake up to sound of my phone ringing. It's the conservation cops calling to tell me that my so-called 'squirrel' was in fact a common old household mouse – albeit a grossly overweight one thanks to all the Kraft slices I'd left lying around.

May very well sue London Electric engineer for mental distress.

Monday   **28 April**

Am currently not speaking to my mother. Clearly terrified I'll arrive in Barnsley this Christmas without an ornamental male clinging to my arm, she's decided to take matters into her own hands. However, like I told her in somewhat harsh tones this morning before banging the phone down in her ear, it might appear like there's a dearth of desirable men when all you've got to go by is the Neanderthals that roam the perimeters of Barnsley but in more civilised places like London, there are tonnes of eligible bachelors hanging around my doorstep without me having to rely on a conniving parent to go behind my back and procure me a subscription to an *introduction agency*.

Tuesday   **29 April**

Determined to prove a point to she of little faith, slink off to the Hippodrome in evening. Ignore the couples snogging under the strobes and scan the place for lone-wolf types. Notice one young hopeful nursing a shandy and gazing at me shyly with puppy-dog eyes. Am instantly suspicious at this since I usually attract more mature-like leers. So before I whisk him off into the night, put him to the test by telling him I'm a detective with CID and can I see his driving licence please?

Just as I thought, he sprints straight for the exit.

Wednesday   **30 April**

Continue to reaffirm my mass desirability with London's male masses. Borrow Eliza's membership pass and head off to her local gym, lounge idly on an exercise bike and wait for nature to run its course. Typically, all the men ogling me are overweight and over

40 whereas all the good-looking ones are ogling each other.

Undeterred nevertheless, press on to Teddington's place because he's having another house-warming party as he's recently upgraded from an unrenovated warehouse in Kentish Town to an unconverted one in Clerkenwell. Sit and talk for hours with single male who seems perfect in every way, until, that is, I ask him to get up and fetch me a drink. Have to cross him off the list too because, sadly, my apartment isn't equipped with ramps or especially low-lying shelves and handrails.

Thursday   **1 May**
Take day off from finding a bonkable bachelor, and instead revisit Teddington at his warehouse in Clerkenwell and offer to drink the leftovers from his house-warming. Despite the fact his spleen's still playing up, his muse is dating a published poet and he's just been fired from the Coach & Horses for carving angst-ridden love notes to her on the tables, Teddington is surprisingly chipper today. Indeed, he informs me that his new mentor, a chief grip at Channel 6*, has told him the executive producer of one of England's longest-running sitcoms is looking for a new writer to inject some life into what kinder TV critics are calling 'an unmitigated piece of dross'.

Seeing this as an answer to all my current problems (meeting a man; making more money; getting Teddington to realise he hasn't got what it takes to cut it in the ruthless world of television), wish my hapless pal all the luck in the world, leave him to continue putting together his carefully constructed letter of application to sitcom management, race home, ring Channel 6, make a few transatlantic hissing noises, affect a psuedo-English accent and immediately get put through to executive producer.

He seems a bit miffed when he realises it's not Tracey Ullman on the other end of the line begging to save the day, the sitcom and his neck. I too am a bit miffed when he maintains he hasn't read my *London Goss* column. With a little prodding, though, he does finally remember my foray into pulp fiction, saying he saw a copy
_____
*The name has been changed to protect the author from professional embarrassment.

of *3½ Minutes* in a remainder bin outside a second-hand bookshop last month. He concedes it was very amusing. It wasn't meant to be, I'm tempted to snap. Although he hasn't exactly got off on the right foot, eventually agree to show up for pre-production meeting next week.

Friday   2 May

Suspect I am soon going to be too busy doing battle with television network executives to keep on top of light domestic chores and minor administration tasks, so have decided to hire a personal assistant.

As my well-meaning mother has already paid the extortionate fees, and as any male would be at my beck and call whether he was working for me or dating me, I'm going to procure my Man Friday from the introduction agency.

By now well-rehearsed in courtship etiquette, tell the distinctly matronly matchmaker that I don't want any man who's too young, old, fat, criminal or unable to take me on long romantic strolls down the beach without me having to lug him about in his wheelchair. Ms Matchmaker smiles brightly and says I've come to just the right place.

I then add that he preferably be unemployed but 'actively seeking work'. She reckons scroungers aren't usually in big demand but she put one on the books because she felt so sorry for him. This doesn't sound promising but, since I'll be getting his clerical services for free, I agree to hand over my unlisted home number.

Saturday   3 May

Job candidate rings this morning. Unfortunately, the plaintive voice at the other end of the line sounds alarmingly familiar. Indeed, it seems that not only is he completely unemployable, Sebastian is so desperate and dateless he's willing to risk the inevitable tirade of abuse I give him for daring to even *think* of calling me.

Storm into introduction agency and into Ms Matchmaker's

office, studiously ignoring the admiring glances from the dweebs filling out questionnaires in the foyer. Anxious to keep my business and appease what looks to be a very promising scene, Ms Matchmaker says perhaps I should tell her what I *want* as opposed to what I don't.

Reel off list of appropriate skills the successful applicant needs, and then, because who knows what will happen should sparks fly between me and my prospective minion, also insist he be good in bed. Upon hearing my last prerequisite, my professional cupid's face falls. She says in that case she definitely won't be able to help and perhaps I should try an escort agency instead.

Think better of it after a quick take on the talent available at Madam Phoebe's big birthday bash at Caspers later that night. Personally, I don't think turning 40 is anything to be publicly crowing about but then again Phoebe has never been one to avoid staring social death straight in the eye – particularly not tonight, given she's decided to pair off a lurex jumper with a mock-croc mini.

Undaunted by the fact that the place is packed with gone-to-seed gigolos and executive spinsters, I seductively work the room, fully aware that all the females are clutching the arms of their paid escorts for grim life.

Shortly after complimentary sparkling wine runs out, make good my escape, content in the knowledge that I have caused no less than five domestics and two cancelled scented-oil massage sessions.

Sunday   4 May
Unable to do much today, thanks to massive migraine caused by cheap muck I was made to drink last night.

Monday   5 May
                                              Bank Holiday
In a brave and desperate bid to single-handedly save this nation's comedy, arrive at Channel 6 for sitcom writers' meeting.*

It should be noted that only successful businesses take the day off on Bank Holidays.

Executive producer immediately puts my diverse writing skills to the test by requesting I script dialogue for the man-hating man-eating lead female character – something I think I shall find quite easy to do, despite all odds.

Think I must be the only woman in this world not grateful to be stuck in close confines of the sitcom writers' room with 15 sex-starved men. Unfortunately, nowhere in my strong code of ethics does it say I have to be polite to members of the opposite sex who are too plain to get proper jobs on the other side of the camera.

Indeed, since I resent having to carry out my allotted tasks with a bunch of loud-mouthed, failed stand-up comedians, give the lot of them anxiety attacks by refusing to laugh on cue every time they open their mouths.

By the end of the day, am rapidly losing my sense of humour which is probably why the executive producer almost gives me my marching orders, saying jokes about loud-mouthed, failed stand-up comedians aren't very funny.

Tuesday   **6 May**

As I'm going to be too busy today prowling the labyrinth corridors of Channel 6 in search of a better show to work on, have decided to enlist a ghostwriter for all my sitcom scriptwriting duties. My Macedonian cleaner seems a little taken aback when I put the proposal to her this morning but then I explained to her that she doesn't actually have to write anything witty because it's for a *commercial* television station. Terminally keen to improve her station in life and after only a few hiccups locating the 'on' button on my laptop, she soon gets the hang of it and assures me she'll have finished episode one *and* cleaned my oven by lunchtime. All for under ten pounds.

Proceed to Channel 6 and spend many fruitless hours trying to convince the head of sports programming that I'd do a much better job of penning live-to-air football commentaries than the early school-leavers he normally hires. When I get back to writers' room in late afternoon, the place is full of ghoulish glee because a new sitcom spin-off has just been axed due to dismal ratings and appalling scripts – which is hysterical really, considering it was spun-off from our show. Within five minutes of the announcement, six newly unemployed male writers are hovering around trying to chat me up under the pretext of scouting for new contracts. I, of course, am not in the least interested as I don't do talentless hacks.

Refuse to acknowledge their presence and instead tap loudly and pointedly upon my computer keyboard because, unlike them, I have work to do.

Wednesday   **7 May**
Head off to Channel 6 to write sitcom (the same one I was nearly fired from yesterday afternoon by executive producer because the newly unemployed male writers got a bit upset after I waggishly told them they were a bunch of talentless hacks).

Upon arrival at the writers' rooms, hear that an amateur sex video featuring a minor female celebrity is doing the rounds. Am mortified when I realise it's not one of my own little *film noir*. The thought of depriving sad, self-righteous and gloating back-drop types who have nothing better to do with their lives than watch a colleague have more fun by herself on-screen than they would ever have off – even if Brad Pitt, Uma Thurman and a couple of dachshunds were thrown in for sympathy's sake – is more than I can bear.

Am also none too pleased that I'm going to have to shelve job-prospecting in Channel 6's corridors today, thanks to the fact I'm going to have to write lead actress's dialogue for episode one again (all because when I got back home last night I discovered that my soon-to-be-sacked Macedonian cleaner is a fan of Sir George Bernard Shaw and consequently left me with eight pages of unintelligible English to translate).

End up burning the *mdnyt oyl*, so to speak, confounding my SpellCheck and trying to ignore the rustling sounds underneath my desk.

Thursday   **8 May**
Today, Gollum – one of my distinctly more unappetising

colleagues at the Channel 6 writers' room – closes his copy of *The Ultimate Joke Encyclopedia*, eyes my *Irony & Satire – Advanced Course*, sidles up to me and, between mouthfuls of spittle, asks if I'd like to go 'toss a few ideas around' over lunch at the station's canteen. Distrusting cut-price food of any sort, tell Gollum somewhat shortly that until he starts ironing his clothes and gets something done about his teeth, to go bug someone else. Fearing he may not have quite got the hint, also add that if, in future, he wishes to steal a glance at my infinitely more superior drafts, to try the shredder because I'm sick of him foraging through my wastepaper bin of an evening.

Gollum scowls unbecomingly and scuttles off, muttering something under his breath about 'women shouldn't be allowed on this show'. Spectacularly unsociable mood continues well on into evening because, whilst I am now a person of some note in this town, I am reduced to attending a party at my former place of employ and expected to mingle with a bunch of B-List types, just so my ex-boss can keep up appearances and impress his ever-dwindling collection of clients with my incandescent presence.

Only real entertainment of evening comes in the scruffy, inebriated shape of former colleague and B&Q ex-minion Sebastian who doesn't actually realise he's not welcome. I accidentally spill my drink over his specially hired tuxedo and he, in turn, deliberately throws up over my Gucci boots. Then, in a last pathetic bid for my attention, he falls over the drinks table, sending flying the eight champagne cocktails I'd bagged for later on, and gets bodily kicked out by me and my sympathetic ex-boss.

Did feel a fleeting twinge of pity for poor old Sebastian as I stepped over the prone semi-conscious dishevelled state lying in the road, but thankfully this passed by the time my cab arrived.

Friday   **9 May**
Spend amusing eight hours watching Gollum fume and froth because the rumour I've spread is that my Macedonian cleaner's scripts scored more laughs than his in front of a live studio audience. Then attend official party to meet and greet our sitcom's actors since

we're not allowed to work with them during working hours.

Of course, my colleagues are here for the free buffet and complimentary alcohol. I, on the other hand, am here for the chance to work the room, get talent-spotted by television executives, be given my own prime-time talk show, then sue them for not appreciating me more, thereby landing a multi-million pound compensation payout so I never have to work in television again.

Strangely, they fail to notice my obvious charms and talents, though I do get to meet with some sensitive young actor types who are surprisingly unreceptive to my constructive critiquing of their decidedly lacklustre performance of my work. Then some killjoy director drags me off and throws me back into the writers' corner which is cordoned off from the rest of the room. (Fellow scribes are all in a snit too because being relegated to the bottom of the telly food chain means that even the make-up artists get served before them at the buffet bar.)

Later, the black-haired, blue-eyed lead actor Seamus O'Hara makes his grand entrance to rapturous internal applause from me and envious glares from the rest of the writers. Assuming the reasonably attractive female he gives a perfunctory nod to must be the lead actress (because I never watch the show myself), decide to befriend her on her way to the ladies so I can find out more about my new beloved.

Unlike some of the thespians I tried to talk to earlier, Yolande appears honoured that I, one of the writers on the programme, would wish to converse with one of its mere puppets. In fact, Yolande seems positively awestruck when I tell her I pen all her lines for her, since females aren't usually allowed to write for the show. She's enormously grateful too that I let her share my hipflask of Absolut, as the three bottles of Riesling brought out in typically profligate network style at the beginning of the night have rapidly run dry. Come evening's end, I unanimously decide that Yolande and I have not quite had more than enough to drink, so we crawl on to some dive in Soho whereupon a beefed-up bouncer refuses us admittance which is outrageous, considering the types they usually let in.

Am not greatly impressed when, whilst sitting on the pavement outside, Yolande drunkenly reveals that she's the show's resident extra, which in casting terms means 'the one who sits in the background in crowd scenes and doesn't say "boo" because then she'd have to be paid more'.

Saturday   10 May
Perennial limpet, Yolande, begs me to go out with her again, no doubt thinking that if she attaches herself to me she'll score a few extra votes at this year's British Academy of Film and Television Awards.

Lead her to my old stomping ground Zilli's, taking care to snub all my former advertising colleagues who, upon realising that Yolande is a guest of mine, have started vying for her autograph. When she's finally finished showing off, I nonchalantly enquire about Seamus. Not very well-versed in the art of subtlety and tact (which, to my mind, doesn't bode well for an extra), Yolande replies I'll only get to sleep with him on the set, since he doesn't go near the Channel 6 writers' room because it's bad for his image.

Can understand his objections completely.

Sunday   11 May
Temporarily leave the heady heights of show business, and plunge back into cold, bleak reality. Thanks to my enterprising pal, Eliza, am stuck behind a trestle table at Camden Market watching my valuable cast-offs being pawed and mauled by middle-class hippies and old-age pensioners. Whilst doing my best to flog a pre-loved Armani original at the never-to-be-seen-again price of £200, it seems that people are more willing to fork over five pence a piece for Eliza's pre-used Robinson's jam jars. A good thing too, since she'll need every penny she can get to pay for RAC Man's ever-increasing medical bills.

Monday   12 May
Am parked behind a PC at Channel 6, ignoring the fact that my

colleagues are ignoring me because I'm ignoring them because I'm now too busy trying to work out how to get on to the sitcom's set and into the arms of Seamus.

At the same time eavesdrop on nearby producers who are on phones optimistically hustling for big-name guests for a forthcoming night-time talk show. In morning, it's 'Bruce' this, 'Tom' that, and 'Arnie' the other. By early afternoon, things take dramatic turn for worse, and I hear 'Geri', 'Bernard' and 'Tinkywinky' being bandied about. Try to save producers' jobs by loudly dropping my own name but, of course, they pretend they've never heard of me.

Tuesday   **13 May**
Executive producer hauls me into his office late this afternoon to ask why I was caught lurking behind a floral couch on sitcom set this morning. He also wants to know how I managed to get hold of a security pass in order to do so since scriptwriters usually have to bang on the front doors of Channel 6 and beg to be let in to do their work.

Give him a disdainful look, let out a despairing sigh and tell him that any girl can get through five sets of Important-Personnel-Only doors if she pulls back her shoulders, sucks in her stomach and smiles nicely for the security cameras. Must say, the rest of the writers seem fairly impressed that I got caught trespassing, even if I didn't get to mate with the main man himself. Indeed, Gollum is positively green, though this could also be due to the reflection from his hideous khaki polyester shirt.

Bad taste continues well into evening when I have dinner at Pizza Express with frost-bitten Ferguson. My swashbuckling pal made an exceptionally pathetic attempt to climb Everest whilst he was in Nepal recently, and is now minus three fingertips – which is why we're eating food that doesn't require fiddly things like cutlery.

He reckons he's a changed man. Since he's also missing half his nose, I'm inclined to agree. Then he starts to prattle on about how he's decided he's to explore his feminine side.

Stop listening and let my mind wander because I've got better things to worry about – like how to make an impression on Seamus.

Wednesday   14 May

After a hard day's slog pretending to pen episode three, head off to nearby boardroom to celebrate the sitcom director's birthday. At nine o'clock precisely, some curmudgeonly station executive comes in and padlocks the bar fridge, curtly reminding us that until our show starts rating higher, all cast and crew are on rations. As luck would have it, I happen to have a pair of industrial-strength pliers in my bag, so drinks are on me for the rest of the evening.

Whilst idly scanning the room, casually ask Yolande why Seamus hasn't graced the place with his presence. She replies he only makes paid appearances and even the enticing prospect of sleeping with me wouldn't be enough to make him breach his contract.

Thursday   15 May

Tonight, Yolande takes me to a private party at the Met Bar. A consummate liar by trade, she promises me it will be a star-studded event. All I can say is if two extras from *Casualty* plus the understudy to a Teletubby qualify as massive celebrity, then I myself should have been escorted in by 24 bodyguards and a standing ovation.

Swallow my bitter disappointment along with a quart of tequila and graciously chat up the first reserve from *Gladiators*.

Friday   16 May

Upon hearing that I am gallivanting around town with the glitterati, Gollum sidles up to me and in a sibilant hiss, accuses me of 'social climbing'. Raise my eyes to the sky, look down my Raybans at him and sweetly reply that I'm hardly going to be able to get to the top by sleeping with him.

Unfortunately it looks like I won't have any other choice in the near future since an ailing cable network too poor to rent a celebrity crowd has invited nothing but a great bunch of Gollumites to a promotional party at some warehouse off Fulham

Road. I, of course, am only going because our hosts are running an open bar from ten till late.

Arrive bang on ten because as far as I'm concerned, there's no such thing as being fashionably late when drinks are on the house.

Typically, about two hundred freeloaders have the same idea so I have to beg, cajole and elbow my way to the front of the queue. Finally, sit down on a chair, balance my tray of triple vodkas on my knees, and cut a deliberately solitary figure for the next five hours of frantic guzzling.

Saturday   17 May
Rudely awakened today by shrill tones of my phone. Angel is ringing to say that, just as I'd promised, filing the divorce application has done the trick and Bogie Boy is now on his best behaviour. Tell her that whilst I am thrilled to hear that he's promised to stop sulking when she scolds him for doing wheelies at traffic lights, I'd prefer she didn't ring me in the middle of a promising dream sequence with Seamus.

Sunday   18 May
Closest I get to the new love of my life is having dinner in the West End with extra extraordinaire Yolande. She tells me she's taken to throwing tantrums on the set in order to raise her public profile. Enhance my own prima donna status by indulging in brief spat with restaurant staff over the size of my bass which resembles the size of an anchovy. Thus receive a second serving which, unfortunately, I then can't eat because I'm too full.

Monday   19 May
Have just worked out that the only way television comedy writers are legitimately allowed access to the sitcom set without being reprimanded by a less-than-jovial executive producer, is when stony-faced directors haul you by the ears on to it because the lead actress is having problems with her script.

Tragically, I'd forgotten that most actors find the English language hard to come to terms with – even when it is placed on an autocue – and therefore had foolishly incorporated words of more than one syllable into episode 11.

Whilst the she-monster of my own creation asks me in haughty tones what the phrase 'parting is such sweet sorrow' means, how she's supposed to pronounce it and what relevance it has during a mock-moving farewell scene, I scan the plywood balcony for my heart's desire. Spot him sitting cross-legged in green tights by a makeshift duck pond, talking on his mobile to network lawyers about financial compensation for running two minutes over schedule.

It goes without saying we neither look at, speak to or acknowledge each other, so overwhelmed are we both by each other's presence. Sadly, I have to leave before my romantic psychosis takes full and savage bloom because I've got more important things to do now, like try to rescue my screenwriting career.

Tuesday   20 May

After making major grammatical revisions to episode 11 as instructed by hatchet-faced executive producer, start to make minor structural changes to episode 12. I've decided that if the lead actress is going to make my life difficult, I'm not going to make hers particularly easy.

By the end of the day, and episode 12 completed, am starting to quite like the parry and cut-throat thrust of working in television.

Adrenalin-rush nosedives come evening, when I have to make cameo appearance at Frangipani's hen's night. Not too fussed about attending an event where there's guaranteed to be 50 women and no men save for a stripper who's got a boyfriend called Brent.

So, despite some encouraging overtures from certain members of catering staff, feel obliged to leave early, telling Frangipani on my way out that I refuse to take part in celebrations at a function room in Chelsea that would have been more at home in Enfield.

Wednesday   21 May

Yolande calls a secret and highly illicit writers'-and-actors' work meeting behind a rubbish skip outside Channel 6 canteen. Pleased to hear from my spy in the ranks that lead actress just got kicked off the sitcom set by the director for daring to question the validity of having to disrobe during a pivotal courtroom scene I wrote specially for her.

Not so pleased to discover, when I get back to the writers' room, that snivelling, sneaky Gollum has been using the Mont Blanc pen on my desk to edit his woeful scripts. Enraged by this blasphemous act, snatch it from his bony white fingers and tell him to go invest in a pencil.

Thursday   22 May

Am at war with executive producer again. Not only was my kindly offer turned down flat this morning, I then find out that the underhanded, back-stabbing understudy Yolande has accepted the recently vacated lead female role that I am convinced is made for me. When I later demanded to know why he'd go for a graduate from RADA when he could have had a born natural, he says because Yolande's a blue-eyed, statuesque blonde who'll be good for plummeting ratings. And besides, he adds grimly, I'm causing enough drama behind the scenes without bringing it to life in everyone's living-room.

He jests, I think furiously to myself as I stomp out his office. He hasn't seen *anything* yet.

Friday   23 May

Have just been successfully blacklisted from writers' room for bravely declaring that I think *Seinfeld* is a load of rubbish.

Race over to the Coach & Horses to tell Teddington that he can have his stupid job in television after all. Am enormously surprised when Teddington doesn't promptly burst into tears as he's wont to do when I remind him that he's a talentless failure who has to rely on me to get him some work. Instead, he brightly announces that he's decided to give screenwriting the flick because, following a particularly fast and furious bidding war, he's just scored a book publishing contract.

Try valiantly not to pass out in shock and revulsion at what I think is a very sad reflection of this country's literary tastes indeed. When I eventually come round again, and demand to know what his tome is about, Teddington starts mumbling something about it being a semi-biographical account of an English female has-been who is hated by all and sundry.

It won't sell, of course. Like I said to him somewhat smugly, there are enough books about Margaret Thatcher already.

Saturday   **24 May**
Still sore at being thrown out of the Coach & Horses by concerned staff yesterday. At first I was tremendously flattered when Teddington finally and very reluctantly revealed that I play the starring role in his soon-to-be-published biography. I mean, it's not every day a man feels inspired to pen a 360-page ode to me. My simpering gratitude soon turned to a rage of titanic proportions when I found out Teddington has tentatively titled his book *Ball-Busting PsychoBitch From Hell*. Like I said to Teddington, as I kneed him in the nether regions, I'm floored that he could do this to me after everything I've done for him.

Between gasps and wheezes, Teddington replied that whilst he is extremely grateful for all my previous efforts to sabotage his writing career and sully his name in public at every given opportunity, he nevertheless felt morally bound to tell his side of the story.

In afternoon, still feeling wounded so march into El Vinas because my lawyer's wife told me he's having lunch there and I figure he won't have the heart to charge me for what is essentially an impromptu social call. After elbowing his more unattractive, male client out of the way and downing his quota of ludicrously expensive red, tell my lawyer I want to take Teddington to the highest courts in the land because I don't like being referred to as 'ball-busting'.

After much reflection and deliberation on his part, and in silky toned jargon, my lawyer says mine is an unwinnable case unless, of course, I wish to perjure myself on the stand. Then, proving beyond reasonable doubt that he is yet another person making obscene amounts of money at my expense, he hands me the bill for our 'chat' and the two bottles of vintage red I've just consumed in my extreme state of agitation.

Sunday   25 May

Am determined to find out which of my muck-raking, mud-slinging friends has squealed to Teddington. Have already questioned my Macedonian cleaner but got no intelligible answer, so I figure unless Teddington used an interpretation service she's in the clear.

Next suspect to be interrogated is Ferguson since his lips are as loose as they are surgically enhanced. Arrange to meet him for lunch at Bar Italia but then wish I hadn't because it appears he's decided to be a drag queen and I don't like being upstaged by a six-foot male in an Akira Isogawa dress. Ferguson denies spilling the beans, bitchily adding that he's saving his own gossip for the press onslaught that is sure to follow Teddington's book's release.

Then storm off to Tottenham armed with flash cards, ostensibly to enhance Katya Junior's literacy levels but really to quiz Angel about any treachery on her part. Upon spying my carefully cosmopolitan state, Katya Junior starts screaming the flat down, no doubt cruelly reminded she's got at least 18 years before she can escape her primitive surrounds.

Whilst my three-month-old godchild struggles gainfully over 'all', 'traitors', 'must' and 'die', Angel assures me she never blabbed. In fact, she caringly adds, for a small fee, she will remain silent during the press onslaught that is sure to follow the publication of Teddington's book. Toss my rapacious friend five pounds because I've heard it buys you a lot in the suburbs.

In late afternoon, last port of call is Eliza's place in Camden since she's decided to stay at home full time to nurse RAC Man back to health. Barge into the make-shift sanatorium that doubles as the guest room and threaten to switch off her swain's life-support machine and rip out his drip unless she makes a full and written confession.

With one eye fixed worriedly on the blips on the screen, and with the other fixed on the notepad I've placed in front of her, Eliza looks shifty but swears that she's innocent. Her brave and daring boyfriend sarcastically pipes up through the hole in his larynx with suggestions that I take some lessons in self-defence since once Teddington's terrible tome comes out, I will no doubt be besieged by masochistic men who like being emasculated by a strong woman.

Monday   **26 May**
                                                    Bank Holiday

Am presently at a kick-boxing class in Shoreditch with assorted riff-raff. Since I refuse to wear an unsightly sports bra, almost brain myself during prelim skipping exercises. Subsequent bout of shadow-boxing proves equally as frustrating, since I'm anxious to tackle the real thing.

Grim pickings on that front too. Most of them are mono-browed cretins who get overly excited every time the instructor teaches a new and more dangerous move. I get a bit carried away, too, and even manage to catch a Van Damme wannabe off-guard with my own deft impression of the can-can. Since I'm wearing six-inch stilettos at the time, he's carted off to hospital and I'm hit with a lifetime ban from the International Martial Arts Confederation.

Of course, now that I'm unable to deter unwanted male attention the legal, non-violent way, have to ring Caligula,* my underworld contact, and tell him I need protection. He tells me to try a chemist. I'm not after that kind of protection, pea-brain, I snarl. Eager to make a sale he volunteers to come round with a whole arsenal of lethal weapons, but I tell him to mail me some mace.

*Not his real name.

Tuesday   **27 May**

Just as my psychotic paranoia is starting to reach hysterical heights, try to bring myself down by going rich-ad-exec-spotting in Soho during the lunch-hour rush.

Immediately spot Sebastian walking towards me, cunningly disguised in an ill-fitting panda suit. Luckily, I can recognise his terrified whimpering anywhere. Whilst I wrestle his furry form to the ground and then proceed to beat him about the head with his collection bucket, all the while berating him for gathering material for Teddington's tome, he bleats on about how he's working for a charitable organisation because a) he can't get a proper paying job and b) he's hoping to make valuable contacts.

I, of course, don't swallow his pathetic lies for a second. No reputable wilderness society would send their volunteers out dressed like that. And no self-respecting advertising executive would willingly part with their hard-earned cash just to save a couple of impotent bears.

Wednesday   28 May

It seems that not only is my agent a professional thief, she is also a frustrated spin doctor. Having just got wind of my woes, she calls to helpfully suggest that if I want to make Teddington's biography look like the pack of lies that it is, I should embark on a spot of 'damage control'. Indeed, she eagerly advises I start projecting a softer, more humane image to the world at large. Am not too happy about having to act out of character because it means I'll no longer be able to subject her to the usual barrage of abuse before hanging up.

Then, in what I think may be a case of exceptionally bad timing, mace spray arrives in the post.

Thursday   29 May

After nearly half-blinding myself this morning when I un-thinkingly reached into my handbag for what I *thought* was my aerosol can of hairspray, proceed to refute any claims Teddington may make about how I'm an environmentally unfriendly, hard-bitten city girl, and agree to go hiking with Eliza on Hampstead Heath.

Unfortunately, nobody told me the place is like a wildlife theme park without the trappings. Indeed, am appalled to discover the nearest shop is about half-an-hour away but nevertheless struggle gamely through undergrowth in my new Prada wedges.

Perhaps unaware of my martyred expression, still-bloodshot

eyes and shockingly blistered feet, Eliza says she's surprised I'm so at one with nature. All I can say (but don't) is the sooner some Arab conglomerate turns this so-called 'inner city idyll' into a five-star resort the better.

Friday   30 May

Good deeds today include sitting in cosmetic surgeon's in Harley Street waiting to pick up Ferguson (or 'Rachel' as she now likes to be called). In a vain attempt to impress her first-ever non-paying boyfriend, 'Rachel' has submitted yet again to the scourge of the scalpel.

As I later refrained from saying to the quietly whimpering giant bandage bleeding indiscriminately upon my front passenger seat, it takes a lot more than a sex-change to convince a 17-year-old schoolboy that a 30-year-old woman is a good catch. Instead, drop 'Rachel' and her wheelchair off at her place in Hampstead, tactfully ignoring the appreciative glances from the juvenile other-half playing with his Gameboy in front of the telly.

Saturday   31 May

Only day three of Operation Paragon, and I've got a wedding to go to. Since I will have to be on my best behaviour and can't cause a scene at St Martin in the Fields, get drunk at the reception or make off with Frangipani's bridegroom at the end of the night, I suspect it could be the singularly most boring night of my entire life.

Settle instead for uneventful dinner and a few quiet drinks at Café Bohème with fellow chameleon Phoebe.

Whilst I proceed to grimly nurse a white wine spritzer for about three hours, Phoebe brushes down the collar of her grey suit from M&S, crosses her Hush Puppy-shod legs and primly tells me that after dallying with the demi-monde she's decided to become celibate because it's all the rage at the moment.

The old me was dying to reply that I didn't realise a single woman in her forties had to make a conscious effort to repel men. The new me simply smiles encouragingly and wishes her all the best in her sexual non-endeavours and compliments her sincerely on her revolting new bluestocking wardrobe.

Taken aback by my uncommonly benign demeanour, Phoebe casts me a look of concern and asks if I'm feeling okay. Reply mock-viciously that I'd feel a lot better if people didn't keep asking me that.

Sunday   1 June
Today, decide to do my bit for people on the breadline and attend party at Angel's place. Having turned up empty-handed in order to really empathise with the poor and penurious, end up having to plunder the ice in the bathroom sink in search of someone else's booty. Just as I'm doing so, one of Angel's government-subsidised friends comes up behind me and breathes lecherously down my neck. Stop myself from braining him with my sequestered *bouteille de* Budweiser after he reminds me it's his. Then forced to stoop to new all-time low and tell him if he lets me have it, I'll give him my unlisted phone number. Deal thus struck, I get only very mildly inebriated and he – like all men who have no intention of doing so – promises me he'll call.

Monday   2 June
Upon discovering that I haven't left the usual mountainous piles of dirty dishes in the kitchen sink, nor have I bolted valuable items to the floor in anticipation of her arrival, my Macedonian cleaner promptly hands in her notice. In barely comprehensible tones, she says there's no challenge to her chores now that I've decided to treat her with kindness and respect.

Before she leaves, give her a big hug to check her back pockets for any wandering cutlery. Did also try to offer her a farewell bonus but, sadly, she doesn't have change for the five-pound note I was going to give her.

Tuesday   3 June
Am finding it extremely hard to keep up appearances in front of friends and hired help, so spirit myself away, warts and all, for a solo sojourn to Zilli's in Soho.

My escape from myself is seriously thwarted when I spy Sebastian the Harbinger of Hate again, this time behind the counter serving drinks. I am thus forced to sponge double vodkas off male patrons all night because I am frightened that Sebastian might spike mine with arsenic. When I am about 33 sheets to the wind and carelessly kissing a stranger as payment in kind, spot my mortal enemy out of the corner of my eye discreetly placing a call from the pub phone.

Instinctively guess he's ringing Teddington about my temporary lapse into full-scale depravity, so feel obliged to lunge over the bar and throttle him in order to prevent him from talking. Later, Sebastian hoarsely tells me he was only phoning the Absolut warehouse for emergency supplies. But that doesn't wash with me. I'd only had 18 shots.

Wednesday   4 June

Mummy Dearest,

I am writing this brief note to thank you very much for the enlightening message you left on my answering machine whilst I was out yesterday evening. Your 'nice little chat' with 'that very polite young man called Teddington' has in fact managed to ruin my entire life – I think warning bells should have gone off when he told you he was a freelance writer.

I regret to inform you that as of this moment I know longer wish to be known as your daughter.

Yours in absolute speechless rage,

Katya Livingston.

Thursday   5 June

Today, my useless agent calls. Through one of her many unscrupulous publishing contacts, she's managed to get her hands on Teddington's manuscript and, apparently, it's even worse than expected. Indeed, she says, unless I want to walk the streets of London wearing a bullet-proof vest and a permanent red face, I'm going to have to counter his claims by publicly disclosing some of my more charitable acts. Agent listens politely enough as I reel off a list of all the men I have slept with out of pity over the last decade. Then she has the temerity to tell me that this is not enough and could even serve to confirm reports by Teddington that I am a woman of 'loose morals'.

After eight hours trying to think of a more humanitarian deed than making 587 sad losers feel special, suddenly have a brainwave. Ring agent back and tell her I sponsor a child in Africa. Delighted to hear I'm a staunch defender of underprivileged third world toddlers, my agent says she'll get on to the case immediately. (Suspect she wouldn't be so eager to follow up such tenuous leads if she knew I forestalled on little Sabelo's payments late last year because I was sick to death of having to bail him out of prison all the time.)

Friday   6 June
Just when I'm trying to turn over a new leaf, it seems that no one is prepared to stick around and serve as a valuable character witness. For instance, in the mail today, I receive no less than *three* invitations to a farewell brunch, lunch and an all-you-can-eat at Pizza Hut.

Am not going to Teddington's brunch, that's for certain. Just because he's flying off to Hollywood for talks with a major motion picture studio, doesn't mean he should expect me and his other guests to sit and eat eggs and hash browns in some hideously embarrassing American theme restaurant.

Saturday   7 June
Lunch at Mezzo with Frangipani who is attempting to bribe me into house-sitting her mansion again whilst she and her merchant banker take an extended honeymoon stroll through the French provinces.

For a minute I thought I was going to have to slum it in the bistro, but fortunately she had the good sense to book us into the restaurant. Eat, drink, then leave my former patron of the arts with the bill, telling her there's no way I'm going to support or encourage her indolent, itinerant lifestyle. Nor, for that matter, am

I willing to care-take the scrappy little chihuahua she's just inherited off her great-aunt Amelia.

Sunday   8 June

Tonight, pay my last vestige of respect to Angel who is moving to Milton Keynes for reasons best known, and kept, to herself. All I can say is it seems fitting I'm being forced to sit in a suburban pizza-parlour franchise in order to bid her adieu. Furthermore, I have a hard enough job keeping my stuffed crust down without her deciding to breastfeed Katya Junior at the table.

No luck on the man front either, since the young and callow youths posing as waiters don't understand the subtle mating signals of a sophisticated woman. Besides, they can't seem to tear their gaze away from Angel's abundance of female flesh.

Perhaps not caring about my grim and green countenance, Angel coyly announces that once the divorce comes through, she and Bogie Boy are going to get married again. Tell her she'd better find herself another best woman after all the worry and grief she's put me through for the best part of this year. Then leave even further distressed after my pagan pal insensitively asks if she can use the pin from my stylish micro-mini kilt to fix up my namesake's nappy which she's decided to change on the table mid-meal.

Monday   9 June
Queen's Birthday

Disappointed to learn in today's paper that, despite having deliberately gone out of my way to avoid her three eligible sons (thus saving her from more public shame and embarrassment than even she could have thought possible), I did not make the Queen's Birthday Honours List. Am tempted to pen Her Majesty a savage note and send suggestive letters to her impressionable young grandsons.

Tuesday   10 June

Having spent most of my long weekend gorging my face because of incessant bon voyaging, work off excess weight by walking in and out of West End shops with Eliza – the one person in my life who doesn't seem to be going anywhere in a hurry. We do our best to single-handedly turn around the retail recession and, a combined total of 23 shopping bags later, sit down for a restorative latte at Richeaux.

There, Eliza lets slip she and RAC Man are going to the West Indies to track down the high priestess and see if they can't get her to reverse the Curse of Namambo. If that doesn't work, says Eliza, they're then going to fly over to Lourdes for a quick dip in the water.

This is the last straw. Sick to death of listening to everybody name-drop overseas destinations, walk into the nearest travel agent and book round-the-world ticket, first class. Then have to suffer the indignity of watching a truly evil south-east Asian airline carrier agent produce a large pair of pinking scissors from under the counter and slowly and quite maliciously cut up my credit card in front of appalled customers. Salvage what's left of my dignity by telling her I would never have wanted to fly in a cockroach-ridden, death-trap bucket of bolts anyway.

Wednesday   11 June
Ring Biggles reverse-charge and ask for a temporary loan. He's presently still in Senegal flying crop-sprayers and drinking the country dry, both of which he assures me are essential steps to becoming a successful commercial pilot.

Indeed, he proudly announces he's just secured an interview with a highly respected international airline. Whilst I personally shall never set foot on a plane flown by my somewhat flaky sibling, I hope he's successful in his endeavours because then I'll get a massive discount on my overseas airfares. Light-heartedly tell him if he doesn't get the job I shall never speak to him again. Biggles replies, in an equally light-hearted way, that this will be fine by him as he is sick to death of me ringing reverse-charge all the time.

Thursday   12 June
Having temporarily forgotten all about Teddington's scandalous

biography, a director from a major Hollywood independent studio rings me at home this morning to say he's just bought the options. Just as I'm about to give him a piece of my mind for being yet another crass, craven male eager to exploit me and my life for financial gain, he goes on to tell me that Bridget Bigguns, the actress they'd originally approached, can't do it because she's come down with a nasty rash and have I worked in front of a camera before? Of course I have, I snap, eyeing the polaroids on my bedside table. He says in that case, he'd be honoured to offer me the main role. Think my ship may have come in at last.

Of course, since I refuse to sell myself down the river for what essentially adds up to a few paltry hundred thousand US dollars, tell him I'll do it if I can also have my own trailer. Furthermore, because I am always wary of strange men calling me up and offering me obscene amounts of money without having first met me, I ask him to list his credentials. He says he's directed *Chainsaw Gutz IV*, *Hot Swamp Thing XI* and *Bimbo Beach – Part Three*. This is lucky for him because I was going to turn him down flat if he'd mentioned anything starring Kevin Costner.

As expected, all my friends are supremely jealous of my newfound good fortune. Over eggs over five pounds at Harvey Nicks, 'good friend' Phoebe points out that downtown East LA isn't Hollywood *per se*. Over pasta pretty pricey at Oceana, 'great pal' Eliza informs me that movie trailers usually come with a roof and windows and don't still have lawn clippings on the floor. Finally, over expensive rations at La Garouche, total bitch 'Rachel' says it sounds like it'll go straight to video.

Got my own back on the lot of them by forgetting to bring my purse.

Friday   **13 June**
Given the fact I'll soon be widely adored by the pig-ignorant masses and won't have to put up with mean-spirited ways of a familiar few, spend part of the day crossing off names* on my Christmas card list.

Come late afternoon and clearly unaware of my new starring
*See Thursday, 12 June.

role in *Valley of the PsychoSex Troll* (working title only), my idiot agent rings to say that she's managed to solve my 'image problem'.

Having half-truthfully told her I sponsored a child in Africa, she took it upon herself to have in-depth discussions with young Sabelo's charity organisation. Thus, in an innovative new move by do-gooder missionary types and a totally and utterly useless agent, rather than me being flown first-class to Africa, put up in a five-star hotel and then forced to pull concerned faces in a tumbledown township for the benefit of bleeding hearts back at home, they're going to send Sabelo over here to visit me instead.

Ring charity headquarters in London, UN officials in Geneva and mercenaries in Angola respectively, and beg them to nix Sabelo's stopover plans. Sadly, they tell me, much as they sympathise with my dilemma (how I'm supposed to captivate and then marry a Hollywood heart-throb with a nine-year-old delinquent hanging off my Versace coat-tails), it's too late to cancel his travel plans as he's already set off from Bophuthatswana for the long walk to Johannesburg airport.

Saturday   **14 June**
Try to forget about the human cruelties and social injustices that seem to invade my world daily. Compile list of requirements I'll need for my trailer. (Not wishing to appear too demanding, have only included bare essentials like eight crates of freshly chilled Absolut, 11 cartons of Marlboro Reds, and a lead-crystal bowl crammed full of multi-coloured condoms with all the blue ones taken out.)

Sunday   **15 June**
World-weary traveller Calliope calls me this evening to tell me she's still in California and has finally gained employment doing some invisible mending for the *Baywatch* wardrobe department. She says LA is full of superficial, shallow people and I should come for a visit because I'd have a whale of a time. Ignore her silly jokes, and tell her that as luck would have it I'll be over there sooner than she thinks, thanks to my new starring role in *Valley of the*

PsychoSex Troll.

I also graciously add that I expect her to come and pay homage at my trailer on set. Following a stunningly long silence, Calliope sadly informs me that, after a year's worth of globetrotting, by pure coincidence she's just decided to fly back to London on the very same day I'm flying out. Am suspicious of this feeble excuse, since I haven't actually yet told her when I'll be leaving. Nevertheless, I suggest we meet at Heathrow so she can buy me a few quick farewell drinks in the transit lounge. She seems hugely enthused by this gesture but unfortunately our line gets cut off mid-arrangements, no doubt by some grossly inefficient international operator.

Monday   16 June

Movie contracts arrive today, express post. Since my solicitor is likely to charge me an arm and a leg, and since I presume he wishes to lose neither for attempting to do so, scrutinise the small print myself. Like most self-respecting, extremely well-paid actresses, am not impressed to discover I may be required to disrobe in some scenes. I am planning to wear as many expensive outfits on screen as possible so that I can abscond with them at the end of the shoot.

Tuesday   17 June

Movie script arrives today, surface mail. Am not brilliantly bowled over when, after an extremely quick and cursory word count, I discover sole supporting cast member Dick Roger has one more line than me. Scribble it out immediately. I don't see why he should get to say 'What's a nice chick like you doing in a joint like this?' when all I get to do is moan appreciatively for nigh on 90 minutes.

Script-editing duties interrupted by call from my old executive producer at Channel 6. Strangely enough, during my absence, his rib-tickling side-splitting sitcom has started reading like a bad *Noel's House Party* script and he wants to gratefully welcome me back on board. Sadly tell him that now I am a much-in-demand film star I no longer do television. However, pass on my regards to

Gollum whom I hear had a hernia after laughing too hard at his own jokes, followed immediately by a life-threatening stroke when the audience didn't.

Wednesday   18 June
In preparation for my big move overseas, sold my car at a garage this morning because I didn't want to do it through the classifieds for fear it would attract droves of lonely old men with ulterior motives.

Later, at some gender-bending bar on Old Compton Street, 'Rachel' girlishly guffaws and says the sort of man who drives a Honda Civic hatchback is hardly the sort to want to grapple with a *girl* in the back seat. Loftily shoot back at her that I'll be driving the ultimate man-magnet when I go to America. Clearly peeved at hearing this, 'Rachel' cattily says she's not surprised the director's agreed to supply me with a Ferrari since, judging by the script I've brought along to make her jealous, most of the love scenes are set in one.

Thursday   19 June
Hollywood director rings me this morning and tells me he wants to talk about the 'money' shots. Since I thought we'd already discussed how many thousands of dollars I was getting per second of screen-time, hang up on him abruptly because I'm still wading through the three-page script . . .

Friday   20 June
. . . first thing I am going to do when I arrive in LA is sack my totally and utterly depraved director.

Saturday   21 June
Think I have managed to beat even the Hollywood system of ludicrous amounts of drafts, rewrites and overhauls, and am at last satisfied that my character is being truthfully and fairly represented. Tragically, was forced to ditch Dick Roger from the script because I don't do men with stupid names and appalling

manners in bed.

Of course, as I am now in every single scene, all of it laden with intelligent non-American monologue, and because I don't wish to spend every waking moment on the set, am going to have to demand a body-double for all the stable, church, temple and crucifixion scenes.

Sunday   22 June
Much to my disgust and utter dismay, Sabelo lands on my doorstep early this morning – without, might I add, the litre bottle of Joy parfum I'd requested he buy me in duty-free. Thanks to yet another one of my agent's 'bright ideas', I'm expected to be 'deeply touched and privileged' to be cuddling and caring for him for a whole week.

Given he's travelled many thousands of miles to see me, eventually relent and let him in, but only after he avidly assures me none of his scrounging relatives are lurking in my flat's corridors. Then, to really make my little publicity-stunt-on-legs feel at home, set him about cleaning my flat because I'm determined to get my deposit back when I vacate next week. Whilst Sabelo's busy with pots of paint, fresh rolls of carpet and a bottle of bleach, get on the phone and promptly sack my agent.

Monday   23 June
This is the last London Goss *diary entry from Katya Livingston. She is far too busy seeking fame, fortune and a self-made man overseas to bother selling her soul for peanuts here. You can read all about it in* Vanity Fair *instead. All proceeds from her new movie will go to Sabelo's family trust fund which this author is going to set up in the Cayman Islands on her way to Hollywood.*

She is sure all her readers – male or otherwise – wish her all the best in her new starring role in Valley of the PsychoSex Troll. *Like her former agent was quoted as saying yesterday, 'it wouldn't have happened to a nicer person'.*

EPILOGUE

Tuesday   24 June

Having already rung my *London Goss* editor yesterday to tell him I will no longer be recording the details of my fabulous life for his tawdry tabloid (to which he dryly replied that if I'd ever bothered to read it I'd have noticed that my column hasn't been running for the last six months – though the joke is on him since the payroll clerk was obviously never informed), am not amused when my accountant calls me this morning to timorously tell me that even *after* off-setting business expenses such as my Versace wardrobe, Habitat leather lounge suite and various vacations abroad against my meagre salary as a freelance columnist and occasional author, I will still owe Inland Revenue many thousands of pounds for the last fiscal year.

Furthermore, he adds, he hopes I'm still keeping a record of my business expenses because thanks to my frank revelations in my former *London Goss* column about him and his financial fraudsters, a couple of tax inspectors capable of reading a newspaper are now breathing down his neck. Thus he strongly suspects I'll be faced yet again with an audit in the near future.

Sorely tempted to fire my non-creative number-cruncher for gross professional misconduct but think better of it since he's just been refused parole again which means I'll still get his services at a competitive rate. And besides, I don't have the time to sack him because I've just spotted Sabelo trying to drag the padlock from my drinks cabinet with his teeth.

Business Expenses: *Accountant's Fee – £5 (as decreed by the newly revised Trade Practices in Prison Act, 2001).*

Wednesday   25 June

Sabelo is still valiantly trying to eat me out of house and home. Since any guest of mine is welcome to give it their best shot, leave him to finish consuming the rest of the condiments passed their use-by date in my kitchen cupboard and the sample two-minute noodle soup sachets ripped out of *Marie Claire*, and head out for dinner with Phoebe at Café Bohème.

Over caesar salads with croutons, bacon, anchovies and oil on the side, Phoebe informs me that the married man who so cruelly dumped her last year has taken a good, long, hard look at himself, and therefore has had a change of heart and decided he'd still like to have his cake and eat it too. Close my eyes through all of this so that Phoebe can't see me rolling them.

Business Expenses: *None. Kind waiter mistook me for a blind person and gave me my meal for free.*

Thursday   26 June
Call press conference to announce my impending departure. Three hours and three hundred no-shows later at the Dorchester, I am beginning to ask myself what it takes in this country to get members of the media to pay me some attention.

Empty the spa bath, put on some clothes and take the champagne off the chill. Then trot over to my old ad agency to gloat to my ex-boss about my stunningly successful new movie career. Now down to a paltry staff of one, my former employer sits at the Gatekeeper's old position at front desk, nursing a glass of cooking sherry and bawling his eyes out, no doubt because since my departure all his clients have walked out the door. As I take a swig from my recently chilled Krug and ask what's wrong, notice a tank of revolting European crested newts in the agency foyer. One of them escaped earlier on in the day, my ex-boss mournfully tells me, eyeing my bottle of bubbly in a covert, covetous manner.

Fortunately, and unbeknownst to its owner, said newt is currently parked under my well-shod foot. So, whilst my ex-boss drunkenly rambles on about how newts have been on this earth for 315 million years and how they're now his only friends in the world, I diplomatically scrape the heel of my shoe into the Persian rug and comfort myself that at least his flattened pal must have had a long life.

Business Expenses: *£1,000 – hiring of hotel room and sundry props for national press conference purposes.*

Friday   27 June
Eliza calls me this morning, weeping and wailing and saying she'll never be able to bear RAC Man's children. Just as I am about to say

that even *I* could have told her that, given his unfortunate looks, she goes on to say he's ended the relationship – not because of the massive multiple injuries and head wounds sustained from the Curse of Namambo but rather because he's sick of her borrowing his electric toothbrush. Whilst privately thinking that some men in this world can be unbelievably petty, try and calm my unfortunate friend down by telling her she can borrow mine.

After poor manless and motherless Eliza's hung up on me, proceed to spend some quality bonding time with my own 'child', Sabelo. Take him into the city to organise his adoption papers and American visa as I figure it'll save me having to fork out a fortune for a personal assistant when I get to LA. Then drag him kicking and squealing off to Doctor Love's surgery to get an Ebola jab. The last thing I need is for him to start haemorrhaging all over the table in front of my fashionably squeamish Hollywood friends.

My dishy doctor says the vaccination's not necessary and, upon hearing I'm off to star in *Valley of the PsychoSex Troll*, offers to give me a shot of penicillin. Thank him in sensuous earth mother tones and politely refuse, telling him I don't do drugs now I've got a nine-year-old's welfare to think about.

Business Expenses: *£2 – McDonald's junior burger for Sabelo.*

Saturday   **28 June**

Me and my brand-new personal assistant head off for dinner at 'Rachel's' place so I can bid her my last fond farewell and also cut current staff catering costs.

Hand on hip, and stubble on chin, 'Rachel' gives Sabelo an appraising look at her front door, and then asks who the father is. Knowing full well it'll make 'Rachel' insurmountably jealous, I drop the name of a tremendously well-known, well-hung, six-foot-seven American basketball player. 'Rachel' tries hard not to look impressed and even has the audacity to question my claim with a disbelieving, incredibly deep-throated titter. She then introduces me to yet another new boyfriend, saying this one's the love of her life. Am somewhat sceptical of this given that he turns out to be a short, pale, paunching, balding, perpetually failed actor who used to be *my ex* until he switched sides in Australia's Northern Territory earlier this year. Wish 'Rachel' well all the same because, like I say to her without bitterness, malice or spite, an overly hirsute harridan like herself is going to be hard-pressed to get anyone better.

Business Expenses: *£2 – McDonald's junior burger again.*

Sunday   29 June

Having now said goodbye to all of my friends (of which I appear to have very few left due to my success managing to breed envy of monumental proportions), receive a call from my mother, begging me not to leave the country. Since our last exchange was quite harsh and bitter,* am fairly moved by her hysterical shrieks and sobs. Then I realise that what she's really trying to say is that my brother Biggles has finally got a job as a pilot with the same airline I'm booked on.

Business Expenses: *Local phone call to travel agent (to book another flight on another airline because I refuse to die at the pinnacle of my career).*

*See Wednesday, 4 June.

Monday   30 June

Sweep into Heathrow Airport, Sabelo following at a respectful three paces behind, struggling with all my Louis Vuitton luggage. As I wait for my final boarding call, decide to powder my nose for five minutes because who knows who'll get the pleasure of sitting next to me for the next 14 hours. When I look up from my compact mirror, spot old Devil Seed Sebastian himself scrubbing the airport floors. Drop my compact in sheer horror and shock at his feet. Of course, since it's all his fault I've just lost several duty-free pounds worth of Guerlain face powder, the Most Failed Junior Art Director in the Known Universe starts hurriedly scooping it up and into the first thing I find handy in my Prada bag.

Unnecessary waste thus prevented, and my name still not reverberating over the tannoy, carefully tie a knot in the XL Donkey Deluxe prophylactic, leisurely hand it to Sabelo to carry, march slowly up to airport's customer complaints desk, demand at length that Sebastian be sacked, and then saunter off to International Departures.

Sebastian just stares after me wistfully, perhaps deeply regretting the love that was long lost in the ad agency toilets many moons ago.

Business Expenses: £5,000 – bribe to customs officials because my thoroughly irresponsible personal assistant was about to be extensively searched, questioned and charged for drug trafficking and I was going to miss my plane. This is the story of my life.